Best Friends Forever

Emily Chase

D0724526

SCHOLASTIC INC.
New York Toronto London Auckland Sydney Tokyo

ISBN 0-590-33238-4

12 11 10 9 8 7 6 5 4 3   4 5 6 7 8/8

6 THE GIRLS OF CANBY HALL 6

Best Friends Forever

6 THE GIRLS OF CANBY HALL 6

Roommates
Our Roommate Is Missing
You're No Friend of Mine
Keeping Secrets
Summer Blues
Best Friends Forever

CHAPTER ONE

Dana flopped on her bed in the Upper East Side apartment in New York where she lived with her mother and sister and stared at the clock on her desk. It was seven minutes before eleven P.M. At eleven she would call Faith in Washington, D.C. That's when the long distance telephone rates went down. She *had* to talk to Faith before she finished packing. She and Faith had already exchanged several letters regarding their visit to their third roommate, Shelley, who had invited them for a two-week visit to her hometown of Pine Bluff, Iowa, but there were some last-minute decisions to make.

As Dana idly watched the clock flashing away the seconds, she smiled to herself, wondering if this whole trip might not be a mistake, and recalling how she got into it in the first place.

It all started at Canby Hall, at the end of

July, five days before summer school was officially over. The three girls had been sitting around their room, talking about their plans for the rest of the summer. They all admitted to feeling a little unsettled, and having mixed feelings about going home. Summer school was a lot less demanding than the regular school year; there were no required courses and the students reveled in the freedom. Shelley devoted herself to acting, Dana concentrated on poetry, and Faith spent most of her time working in her advanced photography course.

"I'm really going to miss my photography class," Faith remarked. She was sitting on the floor, sorting out the piles of prints she had taken over the summer. "The teacher has a way of pointing out techniques to improve my pictures that I didn't know were possible. Then I try them, and it works. Amazing!"

"Same with me and acting," Shelley said, tidying up her dresser. "Did you know that just the tilt of the head speaks volumes?"

"And I'll miss my poetry class," Dana added. She was stretched out on the floor, doing leg exercises. "In the beginning I didn't think I could bear to read my poems aloud and have them evaluated by the other kids. But everyone was very gentle with the criticism. I discovered that everyone felt just as uncomfortable as I did, so we all got over being self-conscious."

"The worst part of leaving Canby is that I'll miss you guys," Shelley sighed and sat down on the bed dejectedly. "How can I survive without you two? I honestly don't think I can get dressed alone anymore."

"Just remember, less is more," Dana said, smiling.

"That's right," Faith confirmed. "If you can resist putting on that extra piece of jewelry, and keep down the number of colors you wear at one time, you'll be a Pine Bluff fashion plate."

"But more than a month without my advisors!" Shelley stretched her arms out dramatically. "I'll never make it. At least working in my father's drugstore will help."

"I'll miss you, too," Dana gasped between sit-ups. "But I've got a modeling job in the Young Miss department of the store where my mother's a buyer and that should keep me busy for a couple of weeks anyhow. What about you, Faith?"

"My sister, Sarah, knows an editor who works on this local paper outside D.C. He's looking for someone to help out while the photographer's assistant is on vacation. It's only a two-week job, and the pay is peanuts, but the experience is decent."

"That takes care of part of August. Then what?" Dana stood up and flexed her knees, preparing to do a headstand.

"Who knows?" Faith said. She tried not

to sound too unhappy about having nothing to do for a few weeks, but she didn't like being at loose ends.

The girls were quiet for a few minutes, each one thinking about what the rest of the summer would be like. They'd been so tight for so long, it was hard to imagine being separated.

"Hey, I've got a brilliant idea!" Shelley exclaimed, breaking the silence. She jumped up and down on her bed.

"Uh-oh," Dana mumbled from her upside down position.

"What is it, Shel?" Faith asked.

"Why don't you two visit *me* the last two weeks in August? My folks don't want me to work the whole month, anyway. I was just doing it to keep busy. And Faith, you said your job is only for two weeks. What about it?"

"Sounds terrific," Faith said. "Can you get away, Dana?"

Dana slowly lowered her long legs to the floor. "I think so. My mother doesn't want me working the whole summer either. My father invited me to visit him and Eve, but that's the last thing I want to do. They'll be newlyweds, and I don't want to be part of that scene. I'd love to visit you, Shel."

"Fantastic!" Shelley shouted. "Now all I have to do is ask my parents if it's okay."

"Just a small detail," Faith pointed out.

"Never fear," Shelley said. "My folks have

always encouraged me to bring my friends around, and my brothers have heard so much about you, they're dying to meet you."

"But house guests for two weeks — that's something else." Dana didn't want Shelley to feel embarrassed if the Hydes vetoed their daughter's impulsive invitation.

"Dana's right," Faith concurred. "Two weeks means approximately forty-two meals. That's a lot."

Shelley admitted that her invitation was a bit premature, but her enthusiasm was undampened. "I'll call them right now," she said, and sprang up from the bed. "My father will be home from the drugstore and I can talk to both my parents. Keep your fingers crossed!"

As she bolted out of the room, Dana and Faith looked quizzically at each other and shrugged their shoulders.

"What have we gotten ourselves into?" Dana asked in a low voice. "Pine Bluff for two whole weeks. . . ."

"I probably can get some great pictures," Faith answered, trying to see the positive side. "All those wide open plains."

"And I can learn to ride Western saddle. The only *real* way to ride, I've been told."

"And think of the catfish and Iowan corn, Dana. We'll have all sorts of new taste sensations."

"That's what I'm afraid of," Dana laughed. "But actually, I think it will be a lot of fun."

"Me too," Faith said. "I've never been to the Midwest and I know my mother will approve."

"So will mine. She really likes me to have 'new experiences'."

"But what if it's Dullsville?" Everything had happened so fast that Faith couldn't help having second thoughts.

"With the three of us together, it can't be!" Dana was bolstering up her decision, as well as Faith's. "But we don't even know yet if it's okay with the Hydes. They might —"

Before she could finish her sentence Shelley came bounding into the room, her face beaming. She didn't have to say a word for her roommates to know she'd gotten the go-ahead from her parents.

"They said yes," Dana said, smiling, trying not to reveal any doubts she and Faith might have about the plan.

"Not only did they approve the idea, but they can't wait."

"Honestly, Shel? They really want both of us to visit for two whole weeks?"

"Honestly, Faith. They especially want to know you better, because . . ." Her cheeks reddened in embarrassment as she stopped in midsentence. The last thing she wanted to do was make Faith self-conscious, but it was too late.

"I was thinking the same thing — that they might really be curious about me because I'm black. I'll bet they've never really known a black person," Faith said, with a slight bitter edge to her voice.

"That's true, but they'll feel perfectly comfortable as soon as they get to know you, just like I did," Shelley assured her. Anyone but Shelley would have tried to forget the fact that she had been totally taken aback when she first met her roommates in Baker 407 in September, the beginning of her sophomore year and her first year at Canby Hall.

Dana, a New Yorker, was from a divorced family. She was a willowy, green-eyed beauty with a natural sophistication and poise that Shelley found intimidating. And Faith, realistic and witty, was even harder to accept. Shelley had never met anyone like her. Faith was black; her mother was a social worker; her father was a police officer who had been killed on active duty in an attempted bank robbery.

Shelley was blonde, blue-eyed, and cherubic-looking, but she felt shorter and chunkier than ever next to her leggy, attractive roommates. Also, she believed they looked down on her because she came from a small town in Iowa. Her mother was a homemaker, and the 4-H club — head, heart, hand, and home — was an important part of her life.

For a while the girls had had an armed truce, but it didn't take long for the three of them, with the help of Alison, their understanding dorm mother, to overcome their preconceived ideas and prejudices. After a year of living together, they discovered that their diverse backgrounds not only made life more interesting, but that their different personalities created a unique chemistry between them that strengthened their friendship.

These thoughts milled around in Dana's head as the clock beamed 11:03, and she got up from the bed. She made her way into the kitchen where she could make the call without disturbing her mother and sister, who were watching the eleven o'clock news on the TV in the living room. She switched on the light, pulled up the kitchen stool near the wall phone, and sat down, thinking how much she, Faith, and Shelley had helped one another through so many ordeals during the past year, mostly external events that they couldn't control. But this trip was something they'd planned, and they had no one to blame but themselves.

Dana dialed the number, and Faith, who had been waiting for her call, picked up immediately.

"Ready?" Dana asked, as soon as she heard Faith's voice.

"I'm almost packed, if that's what you mean. But first things first. How was your father's wedding?"

"It was okay. I'll tell you about it on the plane."

"I can't wait. Do you realize this will be

the first time we've been together without having to think about homework?"

"Nothing to do but wander among the 'amber waves of grain'."

"And avoid the cow pies." Faith's humor was often a little sarcastic.

"That's the wrong attitude," Dana chuckled. "We're going to have a ball. Remember, Shel said the Saturday night square dances are the greatest."

"Providing we can ward off the buffalo on the way to the Town Hall."

That vision set them off on one of their laughing fits, although not everyone would see the humor. The truth was, Dana and Faith felt superior to anyone who hadn't been born and raised in the East the way they had. They were especially proud of their cities. The seat of the federal government was in Washington, D.C., and New York was the cultural center of the entire United States. In their minds, no other cities could come close in importance, and therefore Easterners were bound to be more worldly than anyone else. They knew their attitude was snobbish and unreal but they felt that way just the same.

"Did you get something for the Hydes?" Dana asked between giggles.

"Of course," Faith answered, trying hard to be serious. "That was my assignment."

"Do you want to let me in on it?"

"A gigantic box of Godiva chocolates. Something for the whole family."

"Terrific idea. And I got Mrs. Hyde a challis scarf as big as a blanket with a zillion colors. My mother says it's one of the biggest sellers — freshly imported from Italy."

"Sounds beautiful, but I wonder if women in Pine Bluff wear wraps like that."

"If not, she can always use it as a wall hanging."

They began laughing again, but this time Faith cut them short. "Listen, Dana, this is costing you a fortune and if I don't get off the phone soon I'll miss the plane to New York."

"You're right. Remember, we take off for Des Moines at eleven in the morning from La Guardia."

"I know. I'm catching the nine-thirty shuttle so there'll be plenty of time. I'll go directly to the United Airlines desk and meet you there."

"Excellent!"

"Don't forget your bathing suits."

"That's the first thing I packed. I think that's all we'll need besides jeans."

"What about a skirt for the Saturday night hoedown?"

"For that I think we'll need a *clean* pair of jeans."

"Dana, if I didn't know you better, I'd say you were a New York snob."

"Don't say it!" Dana interrupted.

Then, before they were overcome with silliness, Faith said, "I'll see you tomorrow. Can't wait."

"Me neither," Dana said, and hung up.

She remained seated on the kitchen stool, trying to sort out her feelings — a combination of excitement and apprehension. She was reminded of the end of Mark Twain's *Huckleberry Finn*, which her English class had discussed in depth. Like Huck, she believed she had to "light out for the territory."

As Dana got ready for bed she thought about what an incredible day it had been. She was preparing for her first trip to the Midwest, and her father had married Eve and was off to Hawaii. She wanted to see her father happy, but the marriage still bothered her. She wasn't surprised because her father and Eve had been going together for almost a year, and Dana's parents had been divorced for three years. Besides, she'd known for months when the wedding would take place. But even so, it was painful to know that her parents would never, ever, get together again. She loved them both, and her heart sank every time she thought about her father not living with her, and her mother and her sister.

Dana punched up her pillow to get rid of her frustration and then climbed into bed. It wasn't that she didn't like Eve. Eve was genuinely friendly and nice, and that was one of the reasons Dana had agonized so much about whether or not to accept her father's invitation to move with them to Honolulu where he was being sent by his company for a year. But there were many reasons why Dana chose not to go. She didn't want to leave her mother for that long, and also she wanted to return to Canby Hall with Faith and Shelley. Dana was sure she'd made the right decision.

Eve could never be a substitute for Dana's mother — she was much too young for that and looked more like an older sister. She dressed in such a trendy fashion and wore colors that set off her thick, untamed, gold-colored hair. Dana had to admit she had style, even though she wasn't chic.

Dana wished she could fall asleep, but she couldn't stop remembering details of the wedding. It was tiny and informal, and took place in Dana's father's small brownstone apartment in the East Thirties. Dana's father was especially handsome in a dark blue suit, and Eve was dressed in a short, pale yellow gown that emphasized the highlights in her hair. Dana and Maggie agreed that she looked smashing. Eve's parents — a jovial, middle-aged couple — were there, as well as a few friends, and the judge who married them.

The ceremony was brief, and Dana tried not to show any emotion as her father and Eve were pronounced "husband and wife."

But then Maggie began to sob uncontrollably, and Dana could no longer hold back her own tears as she tried to comfort her. Eve's father handed Dana a fresh linen handkerchief and told her to mop up. Then he poured champagne for everyone, toasted the bride and groom, coaxed a smile out of Maggie, and put on a Frank Sinatra record. Eve's mother had provided an elaborate variety of hors d'oeuvres, and a wedding cake, and after much eating and drinking and hugging and kissing, it was time for Mr. Morrison and Eve to leave for the airport.

Before they left, Eve and John Morrison took Dana and Maggie aside and told them that their home was Dana's and Maggie's as well, and they would always be welcome. Dana knew they meant it, and as she lay in bed, she kept concentrating on that one comforting thought. Her family life would never be the same, but she'd always be able to see and love both her parents. Thinking that she was lucky in so many ways, she finally fell into a deep, dreamless sleep.

CHAPTER TWO

The next day Faith's mother dropped Faith off at Dulles Airport on her way to work. Joan Thompson was just as happy as Faith about the trip, for she firmly believed that Faith should have a vacation. Although the airfare was steep, her living expenses would be minimal. And since Mrs. Thompson had taken time off around Christmas and Easter with the understanding that she would work through the summer, she was thrilled that Faith would be enjoying herself. Otherwise, Faith would have been alone during the day, for Sarah had a full-time summer job, and her younger brother, Richard, was visiting a friend in Ocean Beach for the month.

"Have a great time, sweetie," Mrs. Thompson said as she pulled up to the airline terminal.

"Thanks for everything, Mom." She kissed her mother on the cheek and hugged her hard until the driver in the car behind began blowing his horn impatiently.

Faith lugged her bag out of the backseat and waved to her mother. It was just as well that they couldn't have a prolonged farewell, for although they were both strong and independent, and had been apart for months at a stretch, partings were always a little sad. Faith didn't have too much time to dwell on all this because the shuttle was about to leave. She filled out her boarding pass, wheeled her suitcase through the designated gate, and settled into an empty window seat. By the time she strapped herself in, the engines were being revved up. Although the flight was almost an hour, it seemed much less to Faith who still regarded man's ability to fly as some kind of miracle.

Dana, as planned, was waiting in line at the United Airlines check-in counter when Faith arrived. They greeted each other effusively and continued their previous night's telephone conversation as though there hadn't been an intervening twelve hours.

The trip almost wasn't long enough for Dana to describe her father's wedding, indulge themselves in the free soft drinks and the pre-packed cardboard lunches, settle their financial accounts — they were splitting the costs of the presents — and flip through the magazines. They took turns during the entire flight verbally reassuring each other that they were going to have a good time.

"Well, here goes," Faith mumbled as the wheels of the plane hit the runway. "I hope they've seen a black person before."

"It's not a life sentence," Dana told her. Dana was sensitive to Faith's feelings, and Dana was a little concerned about Faith herself.

"Only two weeks of isolation," Faith quipped.

"It's going to be different, remember," Dana reminded her.

"That's what I can't forget!" Faith suddenly seemed very serious, but as soon as the girls disembarked and saw Shelley frantically waving at them behind the arrival gate, her mood changed completely.

Minutes later Dana and Faith were wildly embracing Shelley who couldn't contain her excitement and let out whoops of joy. It wasn't until Dana and Faith realized that they were putting on a show for a group of amused spectators that they embarrassedly backed away.

"C'mon, Slugger," a ruggedly handsome sandy-haired young man said. "We haven't got all day."

"Oh, Jeff, you just don't understand," Shelley protested. "We haven't seen each other in over two weeks!"

"You act like it's a year," said another good-looking blond boy who was leaning against a post. He was slightly smaller than the other fellow, and wore glasses, but it was obvious that the two boys were related to Shelley.

"Okay, okay," Shelley laughed. "I can tell when I'm outnumbered."

"You could introduce us." Jeff's remark was directed to Shelley, but he couldn't take his eyes off Dana. She was wearing jeans and a plain white shirt, like any other Pine Bluff teenager, but he looked at her as though she were from another planet.

"This is Dana Morrison," Shelley said, nodding in Dana's direction, "and this is Faith Thompson. My two best friends in the world!"

"I'm Shelley's oldest brother, Larry," the bespectacled one said, and shook hands with each girl.

"And I'm Jeff, Shelley's second oldest brother." Jeff extended his hand to Dana and then to Faith, but his eyes slid back to Dana.

"The bags are being unloaded now. Let's help the girls get them, okay, Jeff?" Larry suggested, pointing to a chute that carried the luggage onto a circular moving platform.

Jeff didn't seem to register what Larry was saying, and there was an awkward silence.

"I'll get a cart," Faith volunteered, and trotted off towards a line-up of luggage carriers.

"Oh, I'll do that," Jeff said, coming out of his temporary fog, and chasing after her.

A few minutes later Dana and Faith had

identified their luggage. Larry and Jeff wheeled it to the exit and then led the way to the parking lot where they loaded it into the rear of a dusty, slightly beaten-up station wagon. Jeff held the door for the girls who piled into the backseat, and then he climbed in the front next to Larry who had already turned on the motor.

Shelley went on about how she'd been counting the minutes until her roommates' arrival, and had worked behind the fountain of her father's drugstore all morning in order to make the time go faster.

"Slugger makes the best ice-cream soda in town," Jeff bragged, "but she won't tell us her secret."

"Oh, Jeff, you're crazy," Shelley said, obviously pleased with the compliment.

"It's true," Larry insisted, glancing through the rear-view mirror at his passengers. "I've been working behind the pharmaceutical counter, and every one of my customers tells me how great they are. But then . . ."

"No buts," Shelley snapped. "The secret of my success is putting a spoonful of heavy cream in the bottom of the glass, and not skimping on the syrup."

"It's great for drumming up business," Jeff teased. "Anyone who has one of Shelley's ice-cream concoctions immediately doubles up in pain and goes to the drug counter where Larry sells them something to make them feel better."

"You see what I have to live with," Shelley groaned, but then she couldn't help laughing at herself along with the others.

The banter didn't distract Dana and Faith from trying to absorb their new environment. They'd already been surprised by the airport, which was sparkling and modern.

Larry had stopped at the caution signal that led away from the parking area and turned around to face his passengers. "You want the scenic route to Pine Bluff, or do you want to go straight?"

"I didn't know there was a scenic route," Shelley commented.

"He means go by way of Des Moines," Jeff explained. "Only adds another twenty minutes to the trip and it might be your only chance to see the capital of Iowa."

"Let's go!" Dana, Faith, and Shelley shouted simultaneously.

"You three are like triplets," Jeff joked. Then he gulped and slunk down in his seat when he realized how ridiculous that sounded.

"Not exactly," Faith said good-naturedly, making light of his remark.

"How big is Des Moines?" Dana asked, changing the subject completely.

"About 200,000. That's humungus compared to the population of Pine Bluff, which has only 5,000."

"Really!" Dana said in dismay.

No one noticed her reaction except Faith

who gave her a meaningful nudge with her elbow. Then, to make sure they didn't appear unappreciative, as they drove through Des Moines Dana and Faith took turns voicing their enthusiasm.

"The streets are so clean," Dana began.

"There aren't that many skyscrapers, but the old buildings are so well kept," Faith continued.

"It's easy to walk around, because there aren't so many people."

"And they're all blond," Faith said.

"That's because Scandinavians settled here in droves in the nineteenth century. Now there are all kinds of people," Larry said.

Faith was skeptical, but by the time they had viewed the striking contemporary local art center, the round-domed capitol building, and the city's largest department stores she was convinced. There were a number of blacks on the streets — business people, teenagers, women with young children — and she didn't feel quite so alien.

After cruising around downtown Des Moines for fifteen minutes, Shelley suggested they head for Pine Bluff. "Mom will think we got lost or something if we don't get home soon."

"Right, Slugger. You know how she worries," Jeff said.

"And Dana and Faith have been traveling for hours," Shelley added.

"I get the message," said Larry, and skillfully maneuvered the station wagon through traffic and onto the open highway.

As they sped along the interstate, Dana and Faith expressed their appreciation of the scenery. The farmland consisted of rich brown soil that contrasted dramatically with the golden corn crops. Beef cattle grazed in the fields; immaculate white farmhouses and deep-red barns graced the rolling terrain.

Dana and Faith outdid themselves in trying to sound original. "It's bucolic." "Like a Grant Wood painting." "Not nearly as flat as I thought it would be." "I've never seen such perfectly cared-for farmland." "I've never seen farmland!"

They soon ran out of flowery phrases, and they couldn't help laughing at the billboards that advertised feed for sows and the best kind of fertilizer.

If their enthusiasm was less than genuine, Shelley and her brothers didn't seem to notice. Besides, Shelley was anxious to hear about what they'd been doing for the past two weeks.

For the next forty minutes, they chatted incessantly, totally excluding the boys who had their own favorite topics of conversation. While Larry and Jeff talked about heifers and pigs and who was likely to win the State basketball championship, Dana described in detail the latest fall fashions that she had been modeling.

"You'll love the new colors, Shel. Hot pink and robin's egg blue."

"Delicious," said Shelley. "And what are the dresses like?"

"Just your type, too. Bouffant skirts, and puffed sleeves, and flower garden prints. They have a fairy tale look."

"What about me?" Faith groaned. "I'm not the puffed sleeve type."

"Don't worry, Faith," Dana assured her. "Your kind of classic style is always in. Good sweaters and skirts are in great colors too."

"But what about dressing up?"

"Just wear a fancier material — like a velvet skirt and a patterned sweater."

"Even I could go for that," Shelley said.

Dana was definitely the leader when it came to clothes, and they asked an endless number of questions, including what coats were popular, why were accessories so expensive, was it smart to spend more than three dollars on patterned stockings, did men really care what you wore, and on and on.

Dana was aware of how absurd her discussion of clothes must sound to the boys. They were worlds apart, she thought, and was glad they weren't listening as she described in detail a blousy loose knitted garment that could be worn as a long sweater or a short dress. Just then some of what Jeff was saying drifted back to her. He was raving about a new fodder for sows that was being developed at Iowa State in the agricultural college. Dana knew that even if she and Faith wanted to join in on their conversation, they'd be at a loss for words. She wasn't quite sure if she knew what fodder was, any more than she could expect them to know the definition of a camisole top or a tunic.

The contrast between their conversations became more pronounced when Faith began talking about her favorite photo story that she had worked on. She had been given the assignment to take interior shots of a new French gourmet restaurant on the day of its opening.

"The photography editor was really decent, because usually assistants are just gofers — holding light meters, setting up cameras, keeping people out of the way — but he actually wanted me to take some pictures. And what a scene! Baskets of fresh flowers, crystal chandeliers, candlelight. And could you believe two separate menus. One with the prices, and one without."

"You mean only the person who is paying the bill is supposed to know the price?" Shelley was incredulous.

"That's how it's done with the beautiful people," Dana explained.

"Ridiculous," said Shelley. "I wouldn't order something if I didn't know the price."

Meanwhile Jeff was describing a new

tractor he saw advertised in the local farmer's journal. "Does everything but shuck the corn," he joked.

Such different worlds, Dana thought to herself, *such different worlds. How did we ever get into this. . . .*

Before she could come up with an answer, Shelley was shouting, "We're almost there!"

Larry had swung off the major highway and onto an intersecting road. A few miles and several turns later, there was a sign on the side of the road, WELCOME TO PINE BLUFF, and Shelley shouted, "We're here!"

"We are?" Faith asked, looking around for signs of civilization.

Then a blue sign with gold writing indicated where the Rotary Club meeting would be held, what day and time, and Faith knew they must be in a town. Soon some small houses came into view, and Shelley told Larry to stop going so fast.

"I've got to point out the places of local interest," she told him earnestly.

"Of course," he complied, slowing down to ten miles an hour.

Shelley noticed that Faith and Dana seemed a little bewildered, probably because there was no evidence of anything interesting to be seen. "This is sort of the outskirts," she explained.

"And on your right is our local gas station." Jeff pointed to a weather-beaten garage with a single gasoline tank outside. It was hard to tell if he was being serious or not, but Faith and Dana were too tactful to question him. Also, they were a little afraid of the answer.

"Here's Main Street," Shelley announced proudly as they turned onto a road that did have a row of nonresidential low-storied buildings. "On your left is the fire department, on your right is the post office, and next to that is the sheriff's office."

"Sheriff's office," Dana repeated. "I thought there were only sheriffs in movies about the Old West."

She immediately regretted that remark because she didn't want to sound patronizing, but no one seemed to mind. Besides, Shelley was already pointing out the general store.

"You can get absolutely anything there, from hair ribbons to screwdrivers. It's like a hundred shops in one and you don't have to —"

"Let's have a moment of silence," Larry interrupted. "We are approaching the heart of Pine Bluff." He slowed to a crawl.

"The center of town," Jeff proclaimed, "in more ways than one. The one and only Hyde's Drugstore!"

The store was as old and undistinguished as all the others, but the plate glass windows glistened in the sun. Even from the station wagon, the advertised specials could be seen.

A sharp-faced woman with a toddler in a stroller was standing under the green awning of the drugstore, eating an ice-cream cone.

Larry had pulled up to the curb, and when she saw him and Jeff in the front seat, they exchanged greetings.

"Hi, Janet." Shelley stuck her head out the window.

"Hello, Shelley," she said, and peered inquisitively into the backseat.

"These are my roommates," Shelley told her.

"Roommates?"

"Yes. They're visiting me for a couple of weeks."

"Oh, really." There was a note of surprise in her voice.

"We've just picked them up at the airport and now —"

"And now we have to head for home," Larry said, driving off.

"Hope you have fun, girls," Janet called after them, watching until they were out of sight and her ice-cream cone had melted.

"She's got to be the busiest body in town," Larry grumbled.

"That's for sure," Jeff said. "She's also the town crier."

Their disapproving tone made Faith feel a little better, for she was sure Janet had been shocked to discover that Shelley had a black roommate. She hoped Janet's reaction wasn't typical. Otherwise, the two weeks would seem like two hundred years.

CHAPTER THREE

Shelley's mother, Ann, wearing a bright cotton dress, was standing on the porch of the Hyde's two-story wood frame house when she saw Larry pull into the driveway. She ran down the steps, grinning from ear to ear.

"Took you a month of Sundays to get here," she said, holding the door of the station wagon open as the girls popped out.

"Had to show off Des Moines," Shelley explained.

"That was a good idea, but I've got biscuits in the oven and they'll taste like burnt toast if we don't get to them soon."

"Mom believes in constant feeding, as you'll soon find out," Shelley said. "If you don't gain at least five pounds while you're here, she'll consider herself a failure."

"Don't listen to her," Mrs. Hyde chuckled. Then she warmly embraced Faith and Dana, and said, "I'm so glad you're here!"

"We can't believe it," Dana said.

"Thought it would never happen," Faith added.

They followed her into the house, while Larry and Jeff coped with the luggage. A frisky black-and-white mutt came out to greet them.

"Freckles will entertain you while I help Mom in the kitchen," Shelley said.

The curtains had been drawn in the living room to keep out the blazing midday sun, and it took Dana and Faith a few minutes to adjust their eyes to the dim light. Then they sank down on an overstuffed sofa that was covered in a soft beige fabric that matched two comfy-looking club chairs, a perfect background for half a dozen exquisitely made needlepoint pillows. A brick fireplace was at the far end of the room with filled bookshelves on either side, and in the corner was a baby grand piano covered with sheet music. A television set rested on top of another sturdy oak bookcase.

A slew of magazines was piled up on the large maplewood coffee table in front of the sofa. Besides U.S. News and Time, they included a pharmaceutical monthly, several business journals, a homemaker's guide for the 80's, and a Sears Roebuck catalog. The room was furnished without any particular design, so unlike Dana's apartment in New York which was fashionably decorated in matching floral chintz, and Faith's home which was all Swedish modern. But it had unmistakable charm.

"This is the coziest room, but the town is like being in a foreign country," Dana whispered to Faith.

"It *is* a foreign country," Faith said, patting Freckles' head.

Before they could continue their conversation, Mrs. Hyde came in with a platter of buttered biscuits, jam, and honey, followed by Shelley who carried a tray with a pitcher of iced tea and frosty glasses.

Faith and Dana cleared a space on the coffee table so they could put the trays down. At that moment, Larry and Jeff strolled in.

"Where you been?" Mrs. Hyde asked.

"We put the bags upstairs in the sewing room," Larry replied.

"Otherwise known as the guest room," Mrs. Hyde explained.

"And now we're ready for refreshments." Jeff helped himself to a biscuit, covered it with jam, and picked up a glass of tea that Shelley had poured.

Larry did the same, popped the biscuit in his mouth, and drained his glass before anyone else moved.

"My brothers are always ready for something to eat," Shelley told Dana and Faith. "It doesn't pay to be too polite around here."

"That's for sure," Mrs. Hyde confirmed. "You boys could sit down, at least."

"Didn't mean to be rude," Larry apologized,

"but I promised Dad I'd get back to the pharmacy as soon as I returned from the airport."

"And I have to see about Gertrude. She misses me if I stay away more than a few hours, you know," Jeff said.

"She'll live without you," Shelley grumbled. "You act as though you're the most important person in her life."

"I happen to be exactly that. Without me she'd probably fade away, and undoubtedly die of a broken heart."

"You're spoiling her," Shelley scolded. "At her age, she should be more independent."

"She's not that old, and it's not possible to give her too much attention."

Dana and Faith listened in fascination. They'd never heard a boy be so candid about his feelings for his girlfriend. Probably just another dramatic difference between East and West.

"Gertrude must be quite a girl," Faith remarked.

"I hope we meet her," Dana said.

There was a brief moment of silence before the four Hydes burst out laughing. Tears were streaming down Shelley's cheeks. Dana and Faith couldn't imagine what had triggered such a hysterical response.

"What's so funny?" Faith asked. "We just said we wanted to meet Jeff's girlfriend."

"You will meet her," Jeff promised, straight-faced, "but Mom won't invite her to dinner."

That set off another outburst, but Shelley, realizing her friends were totally bewildered, explained.

"Gertrude is Jeff's special girl, but she's a heifer — a baby cow." Dana and Faith both collapsed in laughter.

"And just because she's three hundred pounds and not housebroken, Mom won't let her in the house."

"I don't have anything personal against Gertrude," Mrs. Hyde said, "but I don't think she'd make it through the door."

"No excuses, Mom," Jeff said, backing out of the room.

Dana and Faith were still laughing when he stopped cold in the doorway, and staring at Dana, said, "I really hate to leave, but . . ."

"But you have to." Larry finished Jeff's sentence for him. "Remember, you have to drop me off at the drugstore."

"That's right," Jeff confirmed, his eyes still on Dana. "I have to drop Larry off at the drugstore, and then I have to attend to Gertrude. You see, she gets fed six times a day — the best way to keep a heifer nourished — and she doesn't like it when she has to wait."

"Spoiled rotten," Shelley teased, but Larry had already pulled Jeff into the vestibule, and he pretended he couldn't hear.

"When can we meet this femme fatale?" Dana asked, spreading jam on a biscuit.

"You can't *not* meet her," Shelley replied. "That's part of the program."

"Shelley has every minute of your time accounted for," Mrs. Hyde told the girls. "I hope you're feeling strong."

"No problem," Faith assured her. "We're used to Shelley's energy."

"I suggest you take advantage of your free time now and relax. I have to get started fixing supper." She got up from her chair and headed for the kitchen.

"These biscuits are fantastic, Mrs. Hyde. We won't need any supper the way we're going," Faith called after her.

"That's right," Dana said, stuffing another one in her mouth. "This is my third and at this rate I'll be rivaling Gertrude in the fattening-up competition."

After polishing off the biscuits, they took the dishes into the kitchen and then Shelley showed the girls to their room.

"Not exactly the Ritz," she warned, as they traipsed up the stairs behind her.

Their room was the first one off a long narrow hall. It was not very large but adequately furnished with two daybeds, a large oak dresser, and a wooden rocking chair. A sewing machine, a pile of neatly folded material on a side table, and a large cork bulletin board covered with sample patterns and pictures of finished clothing designs were unmistakable evidence of the room's use.

"I hope we're not inconveniencing your mother," Faith remarked as she opened her suitcase which was on the daybed opposite the door.

"She was probably right in the middle of something," Dana observed, glancing at the bulletin board.

"Mom is always in the middle of some project," Shelley said. "But this time of year she's more interested in gardening than sewing, so your timing is perfect."

Dana started to take things out of her suitcase, but Shelley was eager to show the girls her own room. "Come see the rest of the house, and then I'll leave you to unpack."

"These are Jeff's and Larry's rooms. They're just like mine, only they look bombed out, and they made me promise not to show them to you upon penalty of death. Beautifully situated on your right is the bathroom which we share, unfortunately, with my brothers. Ever since I knew you were coming, I've been working on them to change their basic slob image to reasonably neat, but I've failed miserably. Just try to ignore their shaving gear, wet towels, and flooded floor. No matter how hard I try, they don't seem to understand the principle that the shower curtain belongs inside the tub, not out, during operation. And at the far end of the hall is my parents' room, with the usual four-poster and a zillion photographs of us kids."

They marched down the hall, and since the door was open the girls peeked in. A handmade multicolored quilt covered the bed and every available surface was covered with pictures of the family. A copper-colored cat sunning herself on the windowsill peered at the intruders indifferently.

"That's Ginger. She's very arrogant, and doesn't like people. Not at all like Freckles. Ginger doesn't like other cats either. She hangs out here because it's the quietest place in the house," Shelley said. "And now for the piece de resistance."

She gestured them to follow her and then stopped in front of another closed door. "*Voila!*" she exclaimed as she opened the door and waved them in.

The girls looked around approvingly at the pink and white room. "Just like I imagined, Shel," Faith commented.

"Made everything myself — curtains, bedspread, skirt for the dressing table."

"Amazing! How long have you been sewing?" Dana asked.

"As long as I can remember. Learned at my mother's knee."

"There are advantages to Pine Bluff," Dana muttered, so that only Faith could hear.

"And what's this?" Faith inquired, examining an official-looking certificate to which a blue ribbon had been affixed. It was framed and hanging on the wall over her desk.

"Oh, that's a ribbon I won from the 4-H

Club for an apron I made in junior high. I hadn't planned it that way, but the judges thought it could also be used as a jumper and said it was the most imaginative junior high entry. It was the highlight of my career at Daniel Webster Junior High."

"Really," Faith remarked, unable to hide her surprise.

"It may sound corny to you, but the 4-H — which stands for Head, Heart, Hand, and Home — is one of the most important parts of our life in high school. I still get shivers when I remember how I felt when I was awarded that ribbon." She smiled with such unabashed pride at the memory, that Faith was a little ashamed of her own skeptical reaction.

On Shelley's dresser there was a whole gallery of snapshots that Dana examined with interest. Dana recognized one that Shelley had had on her desk at school. It was a picture of Paul, whom Shelley referred to the entire year at Canby Hall as her "hometown honey." The "hometown" part took on a new meaning when Shelley became romantically involved with Tom, a local boy in Greenleaf who acted with Shelley in one of the school's theatrical productions. The idea that she could love two boys at the same time was mind-boggling to Shelley.

It was an exciting and painful experience, for this was the first time Shelley had ever dreamed of having another boyfriend. And she wasn't sure if it was only a crush. Now that she had some distance from Tom, she still had conflicting loyalties and had just about decided to not make any decisions about her future. It wasn't only that she was torn between choosing Tom or Paul, but that she thought she might opt for a career in acting. Having her roommates visit was a wonderful distraction, and helped take her mind off these agonizing choices.

Shelley glanced at her watch and gave further instructions: "Now that you've had the deluxe tour, you can return to your room, unpack, and take it easy. Everyone gets home about six and we usually sit down at the table as soon as they wash up. Larry and Jeff act as if they're going to expire if we don't keep them fueled up."

"Can we help your mother?" Dana asked.

"She's already given me the word that you shouldn't help."

"Seven people for so many meals is a lot," Faith commented.

"I know, and she might change her mind in a couple of days. But meanwhile, she's got me." Shelley chuckled and ran out of the room. She had already disappeared down the stairs when Faith and Dana returned to their room.

After closing the door, Dana fell into the rocking chair and Faith collapsed on the bed next to her suitcase. Dana spoke in a low voice. "Well, what do you think?"

"I think Shelley's mom is a doll, don't you?"

"Yes, a lot like Shelley."

"And her brothers are really nice."

"But can you imagine having the 4-H Club being so important in your life?"

"And spending all that time and energy with a heifer?"

"Also, the town of Pine Bluff looks like a mistake. Nothing like a department store, no museums, and I don't remember even seeing a movie house."

Dana slowed her rocking chair and gazed thoughtfully out the screened window that framed a large oak tree. "I guess if you live here you have to develop your inner resources. That's not all bad."

"Or make a big deal of everyday things, like putting up preserves and sewing a fancy apron. Otherwise, I think you'd die of boredom."

"The Hydes don't seem at all bored, so far," Dana said.

"That's true," Faith mused. "And so far, I don't think I've ever seen a happier family. But it's hard to keep an open mind, isn't it?"

Dana nodded. "That's because we're Eastern snobs — born and bred."

CHAPTER FOUR

The challis scarf and fancy chocolates were a huge success, but no matter how hard the Hydes tried to make Faith and Dana feel at home, the girls thought of themselves as aliens suddenly dumped on the strange planet, Earth. Mr. Hyde's attitude didn't help. He was a genial man who took great pride in his family and had strong views. While they dug into the steaks, three kinds of salads, succotash, and mounds of mashed potatoes Mrs. Hyde had carefully prepared, Shelley's father spoke.

"I believe in 'early to bed, early to rise,'" he said with a twinkle in his eye, "but that doesn't mean I believe in all work and no play. From what Shelley tells me, you've all worked hard all year, and you're entitled to some fun. And let me tell you, Pine Bluff's the place!"

Dana and Faith studiously avoided looking at each other for fear they would laugh out loud or snicker or somehow expose their feelings of doubt. They could read each other's mind, and the last word they would use to describe Pine Bluff was "fun." Fortunately, no one could tell what they were thinking, and Mrs. Hyde spared them from choking on repressed giggles by asking Shelley what she had planned for the evening.

"Paul's coming over with his cousin, Jack, who lives in the next county. And then I thought I'd ask Eddy, and we'd all go bowling in Boynton, which has these super new alleys."

"Why didn't you think of asking me?" Jeff inquired petulantly. His eyes shifted to Dana.

"I asked you two days ago, but you said you had to register Gerty in the County Fair. And I would have asked Larry, but I know he's seeing Laurie."

Shelley had told Dana and Faith that Larry had a steady girlfriend whom he'd met at Iowa State and although she lived fifty miles away, they managed to get together at least three or four times every week.

"It's not really a meeting," Jeff explained. "All I have to do is bring over some health and entry forms, and find out what space Gertrude will be assigned."

"Then meet us at the bowling alley when you're finished. We're not going to run away," Shelley advised him.

"Great!" Jeff's scowl disappeared and he

added in an offhand manner, "and don't bother to ask Eddy."

"Oh, okay," Shelley responded innocently, but she couldn't prevent a Mona Lisa smile from crossing her lips. Ever since kindergarten Jeff had been pursued by girls, but he'd never shown the least interest in any of them. Was it possible that Dana would change all that?

After finishing two delectable apple pies topped with gobs of whipped cream, everyone helped with the dishes.

"You take the wagon and I'll take the heap," Larry said to Jeff who was drying the pots while Larry loaded the dishwasher.

"The heap?" Dana repeated.

"That's our other means of transportation," Larry told her. "It's a '67 Chevy that runs on hope and a prayer."

"Don't knock it," Shelley protested, as she put food in the refrigerator. "It doesn't look like much, but we all learned to drive on it."

"You can drive?" Dana asked, obviously impressed.

"Everybody does out here," Shelley replied, and added in a soft voice, "even before it's legal."

"You're lucky," Faith said, and mentally chalked up points for Pine Bluff.

Dana and Faith brought in the rest of the dishes from the dining room, while Mrs. Hyde swept the floor. "Many hands make light work," she commented. The girls were amused at the endless number of bromides that Mr. and Mrs. Hyde used. Faith and Dana began to look forward to them, because they seemed so true.

When the kitchen was spotless, the boys took off; Mr. Hyde went outside to water the grass in the backyard; and Mrs. Hyde sat down at the piano. She spread open a music book and began to play a Chopin serenade. The girls gathered around the piano and listened admiringly. It was evident that Ann Hyde was extremely talented.

"Your Mom's great," Faith said softly to Shelley.

"We all play the piano, but she's the best," Shelley boasted.

"When do you have time to practice?" Dana asked, as Mrs. Hyde paused to pick out another selection.

"Practice!" she laughed. "I don't know what that means. I play whenever I can and Bob sings whenever he can."

"That's how they met," Shelley said. "Mom played the organ in the church choir, and Dad was the bass soloist. Isn't that romantic?"

Dana muttered, "Sure is," and Faith nodded her head. If it wasn't exactly their idea of moonlight and roses they didn't let on.

Just then, Mr. Hyde strode into the living room, placed a songbook before his wife and put his hands on her shoulders, murmuring, "If music be the food of love, play on."

Then he insisted that everyone join in the singing, and although Dana and Faith felt a little self-conscious, they were soon caught up in following the words and music.

They were on the last few measures of "You Are My Sunshine" when the sound was beefed up by two male voices. Paul and his cousin had strolled quietly into the living room — the front door was always unlocked — and joined in the singing. Without missing a beat, Mrs. Hyde played to the end.

When the final note was struck, they applauded themselves roundly, and then all started talking at once — complimenting Mrs. Hyde, telling one another how good they sounded, Shelley introducing Paul and Jack to her roommates.

Paul was of medium height with brown eyes and brown hair that had been bleached by the sun. He had a poised, relaxed manner that inspired confidence, and it was easy to see why Shelley would be attracted to him.

Jack, a blond stringbean, was a year older but much less at ease. Shelley introduced him to Dana, and he said, "Howdy," awkwardly shaking her hand.

"And this is Faith," Shelley continued.

Faith, always on guard against new people's reaction to her, was still slightly put off at his response.

"Your roommate," he stammered. He automatically stuck out his hand which Faith shook politely. But his smile was warm.

"Howdy," she said, hesitantly. Dana's eyes twinkled as she realized that Faith knew he was surprised, but earnest.

"We better get started," Shelley suggested, unknowingly relieving Faith's tension.

"Don't get home too late, honey," Mrs. Hyde told her.

"Don't worry, Mom." Shelley gave her mother, who was still sitting at the piano, a quick hug. Then she planted a kiss on her father's cheek.

"Have a good time, kids," Mr. Hyde said. "Hate to see you go, but it'll give me a chance to do a little vocalizing."

As they headed for Paul's blue Toyota, the sound of Mr. Hyde's deep, rich voice accompanied by the skillful playing of his wife filled the clear summer night. Dana and Faith stopped to listen, both mesmerized by the beautiful music. It was hard to imagine the poetic words of that old romantic tune "All the Things You Are" being sung with any more feeling.

Shelley saw how absorbed they were, and after the song was over and they were piling into the car, she told the girls that they had just heard "their" song. "My mother's and father's, that is."

"It's beautiful," Dana breathed, confused more than ever by the variety of impressions she had received in less than eight hours. First, Shelley's mother, a perfectly contented woman who thrived on domesticity in spite of the fact that she was a talented pianist, and probably could have had a career in music. And then there was Mr. Hyde, whose simple, straightforward manner belied a very romantic nature, if one could judge from the depth of feeling that came across in his singing. Perhaps, Dana thought, it was the less obvious side of their character that explained why they wanted Shelley to go to Canby Hall and have an entirely new kind of experience.

Interrupting her thoughts, Paul asked, "What do you think, Dana?"

"About what?" Dana had been so absorbed in speculating about the Hydes that she hadn't been listening to the conversation.

"About Pine Bluff."

"I hardly know yet," she hedged, not wanting to lie or offend.

"That's practically what Faith said. I guess the one thing you learn at Canby Hall is diplomacy."

"Sounds like it," Jack said. "I've never known any girls who've gone away for high school."

"Except me," Shelley pointed out.

"Yeah, except you, Shel. Holy cow! My folks wouldn't let my kid sister go for anything."

"Your folks make a lot of sense," Paul mumbled.

"Let's not get into that, Paul," Shelley interjected.

"I happen to think it's crazy to go away to school unless there's a very good reason," Paul exploded.

"Before I went, we decided it might be good for both of us. It's not such a dumb idea that we should date other people. That's one of the reasons I thought it was okay to go out with Tom."

When Paul unexpectedly visited Shelley at school, she schemed to pass off Tom as her friend Casey's boyfriend. The whole plan backfired so miserably that Shelley felt like an idiot and thought she deserved an Oscar for creating the year's stupidest love scene. But Paul and Shelley wanted to make up and talked the whole thing out. Of course, when Paul admitted that he was vaguely interested in Amanda Lewis, a classmate in Pine Bluff, Shelley didn't know whether to cry or kill. Finally they arrived at a half-baked plan to let the future take its course, although there were times, like now, when Paul couldn't help voicing his second thoughts.

"Okay, I agreed we should date other people. But the year's over, and it's time for you to come back and finish high school here."

"And not go out with anyone but you, is what you're really saying."

"I didn't say that."

"But that's what you're thinking. We're not engaged, you know."

"Can't help wishing, Shel. . . ."

"We had an agreement."

"But that was for the year and now. . . ."

Jack piped up unexpectedly, "I'm not a very good bowler, you know. Riding broncos is my hobby."

Faith and Dana looked at him gratefully, relieved that he'd interrupted the sharp exchange between Paul and Shelley.

"That must be dangerous," Faith said, wanting to keep the conversation going.

"Not if you know how to fall, it isn't. I've broken my arm only once, and I was just a little kid."

"Bowling should be tame stuff for you then," Shelley remarked. As always, she could never hold a grudge for more than two minutes, and she was cheerful as ever.

"I'm not so sure. I'm always afraid if I don't let go, I'll go flying down the alley with the ball." He laughed at the visual picture he'd conjured up, and the girls were amused.

Only Paul didn't see the humor, or else he didn't have the recovery powers that Shelley did, for he muttered to himself, "Maybe that's my problem . . . letting go."

"We're here!" Shelley shouted as a large neon sign that read BOWLING came into view. The recreation hall looked as though it had been planted along with the acres of corn that surrounded it. It was dead center in an open field.

"We have to rent shoes," Paul said, and led the way to the counter against the back wall where a young bearded man presided.

Shelley spoke to the man behind the counter. "Take care of my friends, please, and give me the bill."

"You can't pay for all of us," Dana said.

"My father insisted. He gave me some extra money for while you're here and he'll be furious if he thinks I didn't treat you to the bowling."

"That's too much!" Faith also wanted to pay her own way, and she noticed Jack was getting out his wallet.

"Explain my father to them, will you, Paul?" Shelley pleaded.

"You'll just get Shelley in trouble, so you might as well give in," Paul said.

Faith and Dana looked at each other and shrugged, while Shelley said "Size five," took the shoes that were handed to her, and asked what lane they were assigned.

"Six," the young man answered. "All the rest are taken, as you can see."

The others ordered their shoes, and then followed Shelley to the last alley, watching the players along the way who either shrieked or groaned.

"It always looks easy," Jack observed, "but I could use some pointers."

"Paul's great," Shelley said as they sat down on the bench and started changing their shoes. "He'll show you his technique."

Paul gave a small smile, unable to resist Shelley's coaxing, and picked out a ball from the rack next to the lane. "You have to select a ball that's a proper weight. If it's too heavy or too light, you'll lose control."

"That's the one thing I do know," Jack said.

"Then aim slightly to the side of the center pin, take a few quick steps. . . ." He coordinated his movements with his explanation and was about to swing when a voice from behind shouted, "And let 'er roll!"

Paul was so surprised that he dropped the ball on his foot and yelped. Everyone had turned around, and Shelley shouted, "You're here, Jeff! How d'ja make it so fast?"

"Speeding, of course. It only took me a few minutes to register Gertrude, and I didn't want to miss anything." He looked at Dana and his meaning was clear.

"Glad you came," Paul said, as he wistfully watched the ball roll slowly down the gutter. "Even though I may be permanently damaged."

He hopped over to the bench, groaning with pain. The girls were alarmed and everyone began giving different directions at once. "Take off your shoe," "Put your foot up on the bench," "You should put ice on it." Only Jack seemed to have the presence of mind to do something sensible and as soon as Paul sat down he started to unlace his shoe.

Jeff looked stricken and raced over to help, and Paul suddenly cracked up. "Only kidding," he said.

"You mean you didn't really hurt yourself?" Jeff roared. "Then why . . ."

"It was my way of getting even with you for interrupting my mini-course in bowling."

"I could kill you for scaring me to death," Shelley said, but playfully punched him on the arm.

"Holy cow!" Jack muttered. "We've been duped!"

"Holy cow!" Dana and Faith sighed in unison. And then they all dissolved in laughter, realizing how gullible they'd been.

The people on the next lane, two middle-aged, conservative-looking couples, had stopped bowling and were staring at their antics. One pursed-lipped woman shook her head and said "Kids today are too noisy."

"We're making a scene," Shelley whispered.

"Yes, Shel, we must pull ourselves together. And I must continue my lecture." Paul stood up quickly and darted toward the rack of balls. He'd forgotten that his shoelaces were untied and somehow managed to trip over them on the highly polished floor. His legs flew out from under him and he hit the floor with a loud thud, a classic pratfall that had everyone, including the couples in the next lane, laughing.

Jeff and Jack leaped up, extended their hands to Paul, and pulled him to his feet.

"Are you hurt?" Jack asked.

"Not that we could ever believe you," Jeff commented.

"Only my pride," Paul said, grinning sheepishly.

"Holy cow," Jack said, "I think this time he's telling the truth."

"Holy cow," Faith chuckled, "I think you may be right, Jack."

Then they all laughed, and Faith suddenly realized how unfair she'd been in her estimation of Jack. He wasn't particularly attractive by her standards, but in the car he'd tactfully prevented Shelley and Paul from letting their quarrel escalate, and his concern about Paul hurting himself was real. Faith always put too much stock in first impressions. Underneath that awkward exterior, she knew Jack was a special guy. Maybe, she thought, Pine Bluff was also a lot different from what it seemed. She might have to revise her thinking.

CHAPTER FIVE

I think you've made another conquest," Faith whispered to Dana as they got ready for bed. The bowling had been a lot of fun, but they were happy to be alone and have the opportunity to talk. "Jeff can't take his eyes off you."

"I guess I'm fated to wind up with a small-town boy — not the sophisticated preppy type, like Bret. It's a cliché, but I thought Bret and I were made for each other. Even though he was known as the biggest heart-breaker at Oakley Prep, I thought I could change all that. I was right . . . for a minute. Then when he dumped me, I thought I would never recover." Dana sounded resigned.

"He may have dumped you, but it didn't take you long to find a replacement while we were still at school," Faith said.

"You mean Randy Crowell. He did come along at exactly the right time. For a while, I thought I might have to go into hibernation. And then suddenly he appeared . . . literally out of the blue. Just the way Johnny Bates did for you, lucky you."

Dana smiled dreamily as she recalled her first meeting with Randy. She had been sitting on a ridge covered with wild flowers, a short distance from school, and was trying hard not to brood about Bret, and hoping to be inspired by her surroundings to write a poem about nature for her poetry class. She wasn't being successful with either, when Randy came charging up to her on his creamy palomino, his golden hair glistening in the sun. If he hadn't been wearing a workshirt with a bandanna tied around his neck, she would have been sure he was a Greek god.

They had exchanged a few words, and then Randy informed her she was on his family's land. Dana started to leave, but he beamed an incredible slow smile at her and told her it was okay to stay. Just before he galloped off, he promised to see her again. And that was the beginning of a new romance for Dana, although she had trouble not making comparisons between him and Bret. The only thing they had in common was their age — seventeen. Bret was funny, quick-witted, fast, programmed to go to college and into business from birth. Randy was reserved and silent much of the time, serious, and not at all interested in continuing his formal education.

Dana felt secure with Randy, but she constantly questioned whether he was right for her. Didn't that mean that he probably wasn't?

"I could never really flip for a local Greenleaf boy like Randy who thinks of New York as the Big City. He's so nice, and he loves working on his father's land, but deep down he's a country boy."

"What about Jeff?" Faith asked. "He sure is good-looking."

"He's nice too, but his favorite subject is Gertrude. That's the kind of competition that I've never come up against."

"At least he doesn't say 'Holy cow' every minute. I started counting the number of times Jack came up with that, but I finally lost track." Faith, even though she'd revised her initial impression of Jack, couldn't help thinking of him as the typical country bumpkin.

"We're being snobby," Dana said, but she was laughing along with Faith. "Just because Jeff and Jack haven't been exposed to our kind of life, doesn't mean they're inferior."

"I agree with that," Faith said. "I should know better than anyone that a person can't help external circumstances. If I hadn't been born black, and if my father hadn't been a police officer killed in the line of duty, and if . . ."

"And if my parents hadn't gotten divorced, I might be different too," Dana said.

"Maybe all these things that we can't control make us interesting," Faith suggested. She was only half-kidding.

"I think they make us fascinating." Dana smiled at her friend.

"Agreed! And since we're so sophisticated, I suppose we should also be a little more open-minded."

"You're right, Faith. We've got to try, anyways."

"I wonder what tomorrow will bring?" Faith asked drowsily as she climbed into bed.

"I know for sure we're going to call on Gerty, and then Shelley said something about a Trash and Treasure sale at the fire department."

"Maybe we could do some Christmas shopping there."

"Probably, if you're looking for a first edition of the *Farmer's Almanac* or home-made tar soap."

"Talk about snobby . . ." Faith chuckled, and then drifted off to sleep before she'd finished her sentence.

Dana stretched out on the bed and thought about the next day. She knew she'd be expected to emote over Gertrude, and wondered what one says to a little cow. She didn't want to hurt Jeff's feelings, but she'd never had any experience with farm animals. She didn't think that calling her "cute" would be appropriate, but she couldn't think of any other adjectives to describe a three-hundred-pound baby. She decided to wing it, let Jeff do the talking, and hope she didn't come across as a dumb city slicker. Having made this decision, she, too, fell into a deep sleep.

The girls were so exhausted that they slept through all the early morning bustling of the Hyde household. It was after nine when Shelley tentatively peeked into their room to make sure they were still breathing. When she saw that they showed signs of life, she sang out, "Rise and shine! Rise and shine!"

"Where am I?" Faith asked, opening one eye.

"You're in Iowa — the Hawkeye State, land of pigs and poetry. Highest literacy rate in America, you know."

"Oh no," Dana groaned, and buried her head under her pillow.

"It's also known as *the* farm state — first in corn, first in hogs, and first in the gizzards of its countrymen." Shelley was irrepressible, and her roommates — continuing a tradition begun at Canby Hall when one of them asked for it — slung their pillows at her. Shelley dodged them successfully, ducked out of the room, and then stuck her head through the partially open door. "The boys are gone, so you can have the bathroom to yourselves."

"Good, I can take my time in the shower," Dana mumbled.

"Mom's working in her veggie garden, but

she left me a ton of batter for griddle cakes."

"That's tempting," Faith said, her eyes still closed.

"Listen, you slug-a-beds, we've only got thirteen days left and if we don't get started, you'll miss . . ."

"Everything!" Dana and Faith finished her sentence for her, popped out of bed, and began scurrying around.

"That's more like it!" Shelley approved. "And your reward for being downstairs in fifteen minutes will be the most mouth-watering hotcakes you've ever tasted!"

"Terrific," Faith said, "and then what?" It was impossible not to be affected by Shelley's enthusiasm.

"The boys left me the heap, so we can do whatever we want. First stop, Gertrude. I promised Jeff."

"Can't wait," Dana said half-seriously. Then she added, grabbing her towel and a bottle of shampoo, "But I can't let her see me with dirty hair."

"Good thinking," Shelley laughed. "You'll never see a better groomed animal, and we should all try to look our best for her."

"I'll bring my camera," Faith said. "Gertrude's beginning to sound like one of the seven wonders of the world and I want to make sure I have a permanent record of her beauty."

"That's the spirit," Shelley said, and bounced down the hall whistling.

After pigging out on golden brown pancakes smothered in maple syrup and crisp bacon, Shelley organized "clean-up" and the girls took off. Shelley handled the car with authority, and Dana and Faith saw her in a new light. Dana had been traveling alone on the bus around New York for as long as she could remember, and Faith knew how to get around Washington, D.C. as well as any grown-up by the time she was ten years old. But neither of them had the independence that driving a car provided, and what impressed them most of all was how Shelley took it so for granted. There was none of the little-girl irresponsible Shelley behind the wheel. She took it seriously.

As they breezed along, Shelley gleefully answered questions about Iowa.

"Why is it called the Hawkeye State?" Dana asked.

"Must be after some Indian," Faith answered.

"You got it!" Shelley said. "Black Hawk was a courageous Indian chief who fought hard for his people and will always be remembered by anyone who knows American history."

By the time they reached Jed Jensen's farm, Faith and Dana had received enough information to write a primer on the state of Iowa. Shelley laced all her facts with plenty of local color and kept her audience begging for more. Her roommates were fascinated to learn that the mayor of the town was also the veterinarian, and that the sheriff was a friend of the family and provided them with pheasants during the few days of open season in autumn.

"It's mean to shoot birds," Faith said. "They're so harmless."

"Not true," Shelley explained. "They're good at eating destructive bugs, but they also have a habit of eating young corn, and the farmers around here appreciate the hunters keeping them under control."

"I would think they'd be tough to nail," Dana said.

"That's one of the problems. It's not easy to kill a pheasant, and they're often wounded."

"Then what?"

"They hide in clumps of weeds until they die."

"That's awful!"

"I know, but they can be the victim of the forces of nature, too. If the temperature falls below thirty degrees — which isn't unusual around these parts — their nostrils freeze shut and they die."

Faith and Dana gasped in horror at the image. "I never knew you knew things like that," Dana said with surprise.

"Well, it's not exactly the kind of thing that comes up at Canby Hall," Shelley answered, and then as she saw their reaction changed the subject. "We're almost at the farm, and I better warn you about Jed Jensen. He acts as though he doesn't like people, but he's really a softie. Don't be insulted if he doesn't say much."

Faith, as always, felt Shelley was warning her personally because Jed probably didn't expect to meet someone staying with the Hydes who was black. She was mad at herself for reacting self-consciously again, but she couldn't help it.

"Maybe you should tell us something about cows," Dana suggested. "I don't know a thing about them."

"Me neither," said Faith.

"You know, of course, that they have four stomachs."

"They must be hungry all the time," Faith said in astonishment.

"I guess they are. They can eat thirty pounds of food a day and drink over forty gallons of water."

"Holy cow!" Faith shouted. It slipped out and they all laughed.

"And you know what they call a sick cow?" Shelley asked.

"I give up," Dana said. "But I think you're going to tell us."

"A sick cow is called 'an udder failure'." Shelley was so pleased with the joke she could barely get the words out.

"That's terrible," Dana said, but she couldn't keep a straight face and the three girls had one of their giggling fits.

"Let's pull ourselves together," Shelley gasped, and pointed out the window. "There's the farm."

"Stop the car!" Faith shouted. "I've got to get a picture of this."

"It is beautiful," Dana murmured. "Red barns, a white farmhouse, and a silver silo shimmering in the sun."

"Hey, you really are a poet," Shelley said as she stopped the car so that Faith could take some shots. Then she drove them along a dirt road that led to the farm, and parked in front of the barn. A large, nondescript, corn-colored dog barked sharply as the girls climbed out of the car. Dana and Faith hung back, but Shelley marched right up to him, held out the back of her wrist for him to sniff, and gently spoke to him.

"He's not as ferocious as he sounds, I guess," Dana said.

"King is totally harmless — more like a welcoming committee of one than a watchdog."

As the barking died down and King's tail wagged with increasing vigor, the girls were convinced and ventured forward just as a craggy-faced, sunburned, middle-aged man, wearing overalls and a cap, strolled out of the house. He glared at the arrivals.

"Hiya, Mr. Jensen," Shelley greeted him. "I hope Jeff told you we were coming."

"Yep," he answered.

"These are my friends, Dana and Faith."

Shelley was unperturbed by his lack of hospitality.

"Hello," he said, and glanced at them sideways.

"Beautiful farm," Dana said, hoping to warm him up. "I've never been on a farm before."

He grunted something unintelligible and Faith thought she had nothing to lose by asking him if she could take some pictures.

"I'd especially like to shoot some close-ups of your cows. Never get a chance to get near them where I come from."

"Got twenty of 'em here. That should be enough for you to choose from." He sounded crusty, but there was a glint in his eye and Faith and Dana no longer found him so forbidding.

"Where's Jeff?" Shelley asked.

"He's working with his heifer," he replied, tilting his head in the direction of a smaller barn. "He's done everything to her but put her hair in curlers."

The girls cracked up at the image and then waved to him as Shelley motioned them to follow her. They came to the entrance of the smaller barn and saw that Jeff had slipped a halter on a young cow and was coaxing her out of the enclosure.

"Come on, Gerty, you got to get used to this thing," he muttered.

"Can't blame her for balking with that paraphernalia around her neck," Shelley said.

"You're here!" Jeff cried, breaking into a broad grin when he saw he had visitors. He tugged gently at the rope attached to the halter and finally got Gertrude to budge.

"Make way for the one and only Gertrude." Shelley took a deep bow and backed away from the entrance.

"Otherwise known as Jeffrey's Jewel," Jeff said, proudly, and slowly led the heifer out of the barn.

"Hold it!" Faith said. She had climbed on a corral fence about ten feet away and started snapping pictures.

Jeff pulled up Gertrude's head and posed beside her until Faith said, "Cut!"

Once Jeff had maneuvered Gertrude into an open space, he turned to Dana. "Well, what do you think of her?" he asked.

"Her coat's nice and shiny," Dana replied.

"Tell her why," Shelley said, grinning.

"I've been giving her a bath every two weeks, and — don't laugh — I use a hot air blower afterwards to train her hair to stand up."

"Really?" Dana managed not to laugh.

"Not only that, but I was here a couple of weeks ago," Shelley continued, "and she was getting a manicure."

"You might call it that," Jeff said. "Actually, I was trimming her hooves with a chisel."

"Next thing you'll be telling me is you

apply nail polish to her toes," Dana teased.

"That's not far from the truth," Jeff said. "The day of the fair I'm going to put linseed oil on her feet to make them shine."

Dana was amazed at Jeff's seriousness, and she was no longer tempted to make fun of him. His dedication to his work was impressive, and Dana almost envied his involvement. The closest she'd ever come was when she'd studied poetry in Grace Phaeton's workshop at Canby Hall. She'd been carried away with the sound of Ms. Phaeton reading her own poems, and when Dana tried to create, she was totally absorbed. Well, almost totally. Usually there was a part of her mind that was always thinking about boys. Watching Jeff now, she was sure he could separate his work from anything else that was going on. She knew that Faith, too, appreciated Jeff's intensity, when she heard her roommate ask about Gertrude's feeding habits.

"Can she eat everything and anything?" Faith wanted to know.

"No way!" Jeff was indignant. "The trick is to have a balanced diet. Of course, I've got her feeding down to a science — hay, corn, soy, wheat germ oil for extra vitamin A, and beet pulp."

"No wonder she looks so good," Dana said, laughing.

"Thanks. Now I've got to work on getting her to lead easily and pose for the judge. She has to stop and stand with her feet positioned properly and her head up, and she has to look lively."

"That's exactly what I was supposed to do as a model — make sure my head was held high, that my feet pointed in the right direction, and that I looked alive." Dana was being serious and she was momentarily surprised when the others burst out laughing.

"Somehow I think modeling is a little more natural for you than for Gertrude," Jeff said, smiling.

"Maybe I can give her some hints," Dana laughed, realizing how ridiculous her comparison had been.

"That'd be great, Dana. I'm going to take her around the corral now, work on getting her to lead easily."

"While you're working with Gertrude, do you think I can take some pictures of the other cows, Jeff?" Faith asked.

"Sure thing, Faith. They're lined up right now at the feeding trough."

"I'll show her where," Shelley offered.

The two girls trudged off, and Dana walked beside Jeff who led Gertrude into the corral. Then Dana straddled the fence and tried to stay interested as Jeff took Gertrude through her routine. When he'd walked her around several times, he posed her in front of Dana, his face beaming.

"She did it perfectly," Jeff said. "Have you ever seen anything like her?"

"Never in my life," Dana answered honestly. "Absolutely never."

Jeff's eyes crinkled, and he smiled at Dana, a little-boy smile that showed how pleased he was. Dana felt butterflies in her stomach, a signal that she really liked somebody — or was it that someone really liked her? She was mildly surprised that she'd had this reaction to Jeff so soon, but she could easily justify it. He was ruggedly handsome, intelligent, and open. But then she'd always been able to find reasons to like boys — Bret, because he was witty and worldly; Randy, the golden boy, who was reserved but thoughtful and kind; and now Jeff. Three guys, and the butterflies had responded to all of them. Dana had never thought of herself as fickle, or boy crazy, but now she was beginning to wonder.

CHAPTER SIX

Dana tagged along with Jeff while he offered Gertrude a handful of beet pulp and then let her loose in the cow pasture next to the corral. "Keep up the good work, Gerty," he said as they started to leave.

" 'Bye, Gerty. See you at the fair," Dana said.

They were making their way towards the barn when Shelley and Faith bounded up to them. "It's all arranged," Shelley squealed. "Mr. Jensen says we can saddle up some horses and ride along the back road that's got some shade. He says you, Jeff, should take us around so we don't get lost."

"And catch us when we fall," Faith said. "I've never been on a horse, except for a merry-go-round."

"And I've only ridden ponies. The last time I did that was when I was eight years old." Dana sounded apprehensive.

"Don't worry," Shelley assured them. "You

can ride Daisy and Meg, two well-behaved mares. I'm a terrible rider, but they're easy to handle."

"That's true," Jeff said.

"Doesn't stop me from loving horses," Shelley said adamantly.

"I meant they're easy to handle," Jeff explained, his eyes smiling.

"Swimming is my sport," Shelley said matter-of-factly, ending the discussion. "Now let's get going. I promised Mr. Jensen we wouldn't ride for more than an hour." She hurried toward the horse barn near the house, and the others followed.

It was obvious that Shelley had been around horses a lot and she showed her roommates how to put the bit in the horse's mouth, and centered the blanket pad and saddle on Meg's back. Then she lowered the stirrup on the left side and asked for a volunteer.

Faith was a natural athlete and was anxious to try something new. "I'll go," she said, and gracefully swung herself into the saddle and then adjusted the lowered stirrup.

"So far, so good," Shelley commented, and handed her the reins. "Meg isn't as lazy as she looks, so just pull her in if she starts going too fast."

Meanwhile, Jeff had saddled up Daisy, and Dana managed to mount her. She held onto the pommel with both hands, and let go briefly to grab the reins that Jeff held out to her.

"Don't be scared," Jeff said, checking her stirrups to be sure they were even.

"I'm not," she lied. "It just seems I'm so high off the ground." She smiled wanly and hoped that he didn't notice how wildly her heart was pounding.

She felt a little better when Jeff was beside her on Midnight, a handsome black horse who seemed unusually energetic for such a hot day. Shelley was left with Red, a strawberry roan, whom she got ready and mounted in a blink. She looked a little like a buddha sitting atop an elephant, but wasn't the least bit frightened.

"You're full of surprises, Shel," Faith observed. "I didn't know you could ride."

"I love it," she said, "but not in the East. It's too formal. Here it's easy and natural."

"You lead the way, Slugger. You know these roads as well as I do, and Red keeps a nice easy pace," Jeff said.

"What's Midnight apt to do?" Dana asked fearfully.

"Sometimes he acts as though he's in training for the Kentucky Derby and I have to hold him down. Better if he's not in the lead."

"Oh, really," Dana managed to say, and clutched the pommel harder.

"I'll take us to Round Pond, which is just about a half hour away, and then we'll come back by way of Black Rock Road." Shelley gently kicked Red, relaxed her hold on the reins, and patted his neck as he moved forward. Faith caught up with Shelley and they rode two abreast, across an open field, while Jeff and Dana brought up the rear.

They'd been riding for less than five minutes, and Dana was just beginning to feel a little more secure, when Shelley looked back at them and announced that they should go a little faster.

"We'll be here till sundown if we don't jog a little."

"Jog," Dana repeated, as though it were a foreign word she'd never heard. "Jog a horse?"

"All you have to do is relax," Jeff told her. "Let the horse do all the work."

"It's not like trotting, where the rider has to post with every step the horse takes," Shelley explained. "Watch me."

She increased Red's pace and allowed herself to be bounced up and down in the saddle, like a yo-yo. Faith did the same, and adapted to the horse's rhythm as though she'd been riding all her life.

Meg and Midnight didn't need any encouragement, and Dana knew she had no choice but to go with the others. She held her breath and tried to ignore the knot in her stomach that tightened with every step. She had this ridiculous fantasy that she might fall apart like a rag doll with all the jostling, and a glazed smile of relief crossed her face when Shelley held up her hand, signaling everyone to stop. They had come to a road partially shaded by trees.

"Everything okay?" Shelley asked, appraising her roommates.

"This is fun!" Faith answered, obviously enjoying herself.

Dana didn't trust herself to speak, and Shelley interpreted her frozen smile as approval. She proceeded to give further instructions.

"We've got to go single file along this stretch, in case a car comes along. About half a mile down we'll turn off to Round Pond where our horses can get a drink."

Dana began to relax and was even able to look around and enjoy the golden countryside. The trees that lined the road provided temporary relief from the blazing sun, and she regained her usual confidence.

"How you doing?" Jeff asked.

"Good," Dana replied truthfully. "I think this is a great way to travel."

"A lot slower than wheels, but it gives you time to think."

"And you don't have to worry about running out of gas." Dana was amazed that she could carry on a conversation, considering how nervous she had been just minutes earlier.

"But our horses do have to tank up with water," Shelley said, and turned onto a path that led over a knoll and down towards a dark pool.

Jeff allowed Midnight to rush ahead, and said, "Let the reins go slack, like this." Midnight bent his head and began slurping up the water, and the other horses did exactly the same.

"I'm dying of thirst, but it looks so muddy." Faith had dismounted and was splashing water on her face, her lips tightly closed.

"It is muddy, but it's not contaminated," Shelley told her.

"Yuck!" Dana said, looking at the brown pond. "I don't know how horses can drink that."

"Me neither," Faith agreed, mopping her face with a handkerchief.

Jeff smiled at them indulgently and Dana and Faith were embarrassed at how ignorant they must sound.

"There's an old story around here about a man who felt the way you do," Jeff began. "He had to make a long journey by horse and the first pond he came to was muddy, just like this. He allowed his horse to drink, but he wouldn't take a sip, even though he was thirsty. After another long stretch, he came to a watering hole that was just as bad . . . fine for his horse, but not for him. After traveling another few hours, he was parched, and at the next pond he leaped off his horse and gulped down as much water as he could."

"He was lucky," Dana surmised. "The water must have changed."

"Of course," Faith said, "this time it was clear."

"Not at all," Jeff said, "the water was muddy as ever. It was the man who had changed."

After a moment, Dana nodded her head thoughtfully.

"That's a good story," Faith commented, still on her knees, "but I'm not *that* thirsty."

"What you're saying is, we're spoiled," Dana said.

"No," Shelley explained, "what the story means is that environment or circumstances can change you."

"I guess that's true," Dana conceded. "Everyone has to adjust to his or her environment in order to survive." She wondered if she would change if she were permanently transplanted to Pine Bluff.

In answer to her unspoken question, Faith said seriously, "I think I've been changed by Pine Bluff already, and I've been here less than two days. You'd never catch me rinsing my face in mud back home!"

"Hey, I didn't mean for this to get heavy," Jeff said, "and right now, speaking of circumstances, I'm getting messages from Midnight that he'd like to move."

Faith started to stand up, but her legs were shaky, and she had to lean against Meg in order to regain her balance. The world spun for a moment, and she clutched the saddle as she tried to steady herself.

"You okay?" Jeff asked, sliding out of his saddle. He looped Midnight's reins around a small hickory tree and ran to Faith.

"Sure, I'm fine," she answered. "I just stood up too quickly. It's the heat, I guess."

"Put your knee here," Jeff ordered, cupping his hands together. "I'll give you a boost."

Faith did what she was told, and once she was settled in the saddle, her dizziness faded.

"You're sure you're okay, Faith? I don't want to be responsible for you doing something dramatic like falling off a horse and breaking a leg." Shelley was only half-kidding.

"Honest, I'm fine," she insisted. "Which way do we go?"

"This way," Shelley said, taking the lead and heading up the knoll.

Once they had reached the top and were descending, all four horses picked up speed. Dana momentarily lost control of Daisy, who bolted ahead.

"Help!" Dana gasped, as Daisy rushed past the others.

"Pull the reins, pull the reins," Shelley yelled when she realized what was happening.

"Don't let her go on the road," Faith shouted. "Stop her!"

"I can't," Dana screamed. She had let go of the reins and was clutching the pommel so hard with both hands that her knuckles had turned white.

"She's heading for the road!" Shelley shrieked.

"She can get killed!" Faith shouted.

"Help me! Dana cried, her voice trembling with fear. She was going at such a fast clip, her feet dangling loose from the stirrups, and her body swerving to one side at such a bizarre angle, that it was a miracle she didn't fall.

"Hang on, Dana," Jeff encouraged her. Then he leaned forward in his saddle, gave Midnight his head, and allowed him to charge forward until he had caught up with Daisy.

Faith and Shelley watched in terror as Daisy and Midnight came within a foot of the road.

"I hope a car isn't coming." Faith spoke in a low voice, almost like she was praying.

"I can't look," Shelley groaned, and covered her eyes with her hand.

Then, miraculously, and with total disregard for his own safety, Jeff leaned half-way out of his saddle. Using all his strength, he jerked Midnight's reins and simultaneously grabbed Daisy's which were flopping on her neck. He yanked them as hard as he could, and then skillfully maneuvered his horse in front of Daisy so that there was no way she could pass him.

"Thank you, Jeff, thank you," Dana murmured. She was shaken, but so grateful that she had been rescued, she could barely speak.

She looked at Jeff lovingly, and hoped he could read in her eyes her enormous gratitude.

Jeff returned her glance, and that crinkly smile around his eyes told her that he understood . . . that some things are beyond words.

"I think you saved my life, Jeff," she said. Even those dramatic words sounded trite, compared to how she was feeling.

"Don't be silly," he responded, his face getting crimson with embarrassment.

"Yeah," Shelley offered, as she and Faith walked their horses towards them, "the worst that could happen is you'd be hit by a car or thrown a few feet into the air."

"Nothing serious," Faith remarked. She, too, wanted to make light of the incident. "Now you've got something to write home about."

"I can think of better things," Dana sighed, holding tightly on the reins that Jeff handed her.

"As a matter of fact, I don't think we should tell anyone about this." Shelley was being serious. "Mr. Jensen will be sorry he let us take out the horses, and my folks will think I'm not taking good care of you."

"Shelley's right," Dana agreed. "I'd just as soon not have this featured in the *Pine Bluff Gazette*."

"I can see the headline now," Shelley joked. " 'Visitor from the East Taken for a Ride.' "

Just then a jeep came tooling down the road and slowed up as it approached the riders. A bespectacled, gray-haired woman peered at the group and then waved frantically when she recognized Shelley and Jeff. "Howdy, Hydes," she greeted them. "Your Mom told me you were having visitors."

"Howdy, Mrs. Claxton," Shelley said.

"It's good to see nice young people having a nice peaceful ride."

"Sure is," Jeff managed to say without choking.

"Say hello to your folks for me, will you?" Without waiting for an answer, she drove off, and when she was a safe distance away the four of them burst out laughing.

"We're lucky on our timing," Shelley said between giggles. "Mrs. Claxton is part of my mother's bridge club. She's a sweet lady but she reports everything. Minutes earlier and she'd be calling us anything but 'nice young people having a nice peaceful ride.' "

"Let's get going," Jeff said. "Midnight is getting impatient."

"Fall in line, guys, while we cross the road," Shelley directed. "Then we can lope across the field until we hit Black Rock."

"Loping is like being in a rocking chair," Jeff explained when he saw Faith's and Dana's raised-eyebrow look. "It's a little faster than a jog, but easier. Are you up for it?"

"Sure," Dana croaked, not wanting to be a bad sport. Then, as Shelley and Jeff started across the road, she whispered to Faith, "I take back anything I ever said about being bored in Iowa."

"Me too," Faith murmured. "So far it's been fun and games every minute."

"Not to say hair-raising."

"And it's only the beginning."

"Jeff was a hero," Faith said. "He reminded me a little of Johnny — the same kind of cool in a crisis."

Faith was referring to the time that she and her boyfriend, Johnny, along with a number of other customers, were held hostage in the Tutti Frutti Ice Cream Parlor in Greenleaf. It was Johnny's quick thinking and action that enabled the police to capture the two gunmen.

"You're right," Dana said, and the butterflies started going berserk as she thought of Jeff saving her from what might have been a tragedy.

"Hiya Dad, hiya Larry," Shelley shouted the minute she burst into the drugstore with Dana and Faith.

Larry had just finished with a customer, and Mr. Hyde was poring over a prescription. They were both standing behind the drug counter.

"Been expecting you," Mr. Hyde said.

"I assured Dad you'd make it by lunch-time," Larry remarked.

"I could eat a horse," Shelley piped up.

"Just as well you didn't say that around Daisy," Dana said. "No telling what she might have done."

"Did you meet Gertrude?" Mr. Hyde asked.

"Met Gertrude, and went riding," Faith told him. She was still feeling light-headed from all the excitement.

"Then you must be starved. Have Tad fix you whatever you want. Treat's on me, of course."

"Thanks, Dad. Will you sit with us?" Shelley asked.

" 'Fraid not. I have to work on these pre-scriptions. They're going to be picked up later this afternoon."

"How about you, Larry?"

"I've got to man the counter, Slugger. May-be I can interest you in an all-in-one vitamin pill. We just got a new shipment."

"No offense, but I think we prefer a sand-wich." Shelley turned to Dana and Faith. "Come put in your order, and then you can check out the store and keep an eye on Larry while I help Tad."

"See you later, girls," Mr. Hyde said, and disappeared into a back room.

Dana and Faith followed Shelley to the fountain, studied the menu, and ordered sandwiches and ice cream sodas from Tad.

He was a rosy-cheeked boy whom Shelley introduced as one of her oldest friends.

"We met in kindergarten," Tad said. "Shelley showed me how to build blocks the first day of school, and just last week she taught me how to make ice cream sodas."

Shelley had gone around the counter and was washing her hands in the sink. "Now he makes them almost as good as I do," she admitted, "but today I'll do the honors. You guys can wander around while we get everything ready. Larry will be disappointed if you don't buy something from him."

Dana and Faith were both grateful for the opportunity to buy something. Dana didn't want to make a big deal about her hands, but she knew it would be wise to protect them with some Band-Aids. And Faith wanted to buy something for the weird feeling in her head. Neither of them wanted to mention their problems, so they casually ambled around the store, checking out the merchandise displayed in the old-fashioned glass cases. They zeroed in on the cosmetic counter, which offered such a limited number of items that they couldn't help being surprised.

Larry had just finished with a customer, when Shelley shouted from the fountain, "You have exactly three minutes to buy something and make Larry happy."

"You don't have to listen to my kid sister," Larry grinned.

"As a matter of fact, I could use a box of Band-Aids," Dana said in an offhand manner, as she and Faith ambled over to the pharmaceutical counter.

"And I'd like a bottle of aspirin," Faith said.

"I've never heard of anything so unimaginative," Shelley exclaimed when she heard their requests.

"You stick to your fountain," Larry said, handing the girls their orders. "This is my department."

"We're ready for you," Shelley said, spooning a dollop of whipped cream on top of each soda. Then she zoomed to the other side of the counter, and sat down on a stool while her roommates won the argument with Larry about who should pay for their purchases.

Dana and Shelley dove into their sandwiches as though they hadn't eaten in days, while Faith took a few tentative bites and then put it down. She managed to drink her soda and was grateful that no one noticed when she popped an aspirin into her mouth.

"I think we've had enough physical activity for today," Shelley decided. "But this is a good time to take in the stores — I mean store. Next door is the general store and you can see what the well-dressed Pine Bluffian wears."

"Country western is very big in clothes," Dana said. "And here we're at the source."

"Between the general store and Hyde's

Drugstore," Shelley bragged, "you can have anything you want or need in Pine Bluff — or for that matter, in the whole United States!"

Dana recalled Larry's description of Hyde's Drugstore when they passed it the first time. It seemed to her like an exaggeration, but now she believed it.

"Larry wasn't kidding when he called this 'the heart of Pine Bluff'," she remarked.

"For sure," Shelley said, and smiled proudly while Dana and Faith exchanged a meaningful look.

CHAPTER SEVEN

The general store was a rambling wreck haphazardly divided into sections. It took several seconds to adjust to the dimly lit aisles after coming in from the brilliant afternoon sun, and Dana and Faith stood just inside the door blinking. Once they could focus their eyes, they gaped in awe at the variety of goods — bolts of cloth stuffed onto shelves, baskets hanging from the ceiling, barrels loaded with coffee beans, mason jars filled with candy, and every conceivable household utensil or gadget scattered across the counters.

"What a mess," Dana muttered without thinking.

"How do you find anything here?" Faith asked.

Shelley laughed at their bewilderment. "You get used to it, I guess. I think it's kind of cozy."

Dana and Faith looked at her as though

she'd flipped out, but didn't give her an argument.

"I have to buy some yarn," Shelley said, "and then I'll meet you at the clothes rack."

"Could you give us a clue as to where that might be?" Dana asked.

"At the back of the store, on the right, past the goldfish and turtles."

"Goldfish and turtles!" they repeated.

"Who are your friends, Shelley?" A crisp voice came from behind a counter several feet from where they were standing.

"Oh, hi, Lily. These are my roommates from school, Dana and Faith."

"I guess you girls from the East don't know about general stores." Lily was a plain-looking middle-aged woman with straight gray hair, no make-up, and wearing a pale denim dress. Her manner was indignant and Dana was afraid she had offended her.

"You're right," Dana admitted. "I've never been to one before. It's kind of wonderful."

"It is different," Faith said, "and I can see the advantages of having everything on one floor."

"Frankly, I don't know how you can stand shopping in those monstrous department stores. I was in one three years ago, and talk about not finding anything! I needed radar and a St. Bernard to find my way out! Never again."

"I never thought about it that way," Dana confessed, and wondered what Lily would think if she knew her mother was a buyer and that she, Dana, had been working in a department store for the past couple of weeks. She was glad there was no reason for her to tell her when Shelley blurted out, "Dana's mother is a buyer for one of New York's biggest department stores, and Dana was a model there just before she came here."

"Is that so?" Lily looked at Dana, shook her head, and then went back to picking up what seemed like hundreds of unmatched buttons that had spilled out of a basket onto the floor.

"I have to find a skein of purple yarn to trim the sweater I'm making, and my friends want to look at the clothes," Shelley said.

"That's what we're here for," Lily stated without looking up. "If you see anything you want, let me know."

Shelley went to the wool section while Dana and Faith wended their way to the back of the store. "Lily doesn't seem too anxious to sell us anything," Dana whispered.

"I guess that laid back manner is typical in Pine Bluff." Faith, too, kept her voice low.

"It is nice to know that we can browse without . . ." Dana started to say, but then they both let out a shriek.

"What's the trouble, girls?" Lily asked calmly. "Did you see our resident mouse? Friendly fellow, but he doesn't usually come out in the day."

Shelley had darted down the aisle to see what was happening. "Not a mouse, an alligator," she roared, picking up by the tail one of several small dried stuffed alligators from the counter.

"They look so real," Dana exclaimed.

"Perfect for my kid brother. I promised I'd bring him a souvenir," Faith said gleefully.

"Not typical from these parts," Lily told her, almost as though she were trying hard *not* to make the sale. "They're imported from the Everglades."

"That's okay," Faith assured her, "he'll love it."

"If you say so . . . but it's not what I'd call a souvenir," Lily mumbled.

Faith and Dana exchanged one of their "it takes all kinds" looks and continued down the aisle.

"I think this is the clothes department," Dana tittered softly, as they approached two racks of clothes. One was obviously for men, with jeans and overalls, and lumber jackets jammed together. An array of women's garments hung from the other.

"I have just the frock for you," Faith giggled as she removed a frilly jumper from the rack and held it up to her. "This is you, Dana."

"Thanks a lot," Dana groaned, and grabbed a wildly flowered blouse. "And this is *you*," she retaliated.

Then they outdid themselves making fun of the clothes and finding suitably colorful adjectives to describe them.

They were cracking up with silliness when Shelley came running over. "What's ailing you?" she asked.

"These clothes," Dana answered.

"They're too much," said Faith.

"I had a feeling you wouldn't find what you wanted," Shelley said.

"Must be one of the challenges of living in Pine Bluff," Faith said sarcastically.

"You don't have to be in a big city to buy good clothes. A lot of people manage to dress well here," Shelley retorted. There was an edge to her voice.

"I'm sure they do," Faith said quickly. She knew her snobbiness had surfaced and she wanted to make amends.

"Besides, I make most of my clothes," Shelley reminded her.

"And you're the best!" Dana wanted to re-assure Shelley and also rescue Faith.

"Magic fingers," Faith said, easing the tension, and making Shelley smile.

"Did you find what you wanted, Shel?" Dana asked.

"I found just the right shade of purple wool, so we can go now if you've had enough," Shelley said.

"Not nearly," Dana replied. "We've barely scratched the surface."

"But we've got to go to the Trash and

Treasure sale. That only lasts a day and we can always come back. Pick out your alligator, Faith, and let's go."

"If you say so," Faith agreed reluctantly. She walked over to the alligator counter, and made her selection.

Lily was grumpy as ever as she wrote up the sales for the wool and the alligator.

"It's not going to bite," she growled as Faith gingerly handed it to her.

"Just stick it in a bag," Faith said.

"It's a present, isn't it?" Lily snapped, and proceeded to tie an elaborate red ribbon around its neck. Then she wrapped it in an unusual speckled paper.

"That's perfect," Faith said. "I never thought of dressing up an alligator." She handed her a five-dollar bill.

"Humph, you people from the East," Lily muttered, as she gave her the change.

"We loved seeing your store," Dana said, as they started to leave. "And I'm sure we'll be back."

"I'm always here," Lily said matter-of-factly, and gave the girls their packages. Then she turned away and continued her button project.

The girls called good-bye as they headed for the door but Lily didn't bother to respond.

"That's a new kind of merchandising," Dana remarked as they climbed into the car. "How does she stay in business?"

"If you're the only store in town, it's easy," Shelley said.

"But she's not what you'd call friendly," Faith commented.

"She's a little afraid of anyone who lives east of Kalamazoo."

"At least it's super to be in a store where no one cares whether they make a sale or not." Dana was thinking of some of the salespersons she met in New York who would kill for a commission.

"Especially when there's nothing you want to buy," Shelley said, laughing, "except an alligator."

"I think there may have been a lot of hidden goodies there," Faith said.

"If you think that, wait'll you see what's coming up."

Shelley drove a few blocks and parked the car across from the fire department where dozens of people were milling around outdoor booths. She got out, saying, "I'll let you loose and meet you back at the car in exactly one hour. We should beat my brothers home so we can take showers without interference. Tonight's the hayride and we don't want anyone to mistake us for a horse or cow."

The girls agreed, synchronized their watches, and ran across the road. Shelley immediately got involved talking to the fire chief who was leaning against the front of the building and acting as official greeter.

Dana and Faith took off just as he was telling Shelley to tell her father how the new medicine had helped his mother's arthritis.

"Fingers are so good now, she can go back to sewing," he said.

"I'm so glad. . . ." Shelley responded.

When they were a safe distance away, Dana said, "The Hydes must know about everyone's state of health in the entire town."

"Personally, I don't think it's anyone's business." Faith sounded testy, and Dana was surprised at her friend's reaction.

"You mean if you had arthritis, you wouldn't want your son to talk about it."

"Exactly." Faith couldn't help laughing at the absurdity and was grateful that Dana hadn't asked her what was bugging her. The last thing she wanted to do was admit that she felt at all sick, but she knew something was wrong. She felt weak and headachey, but decided to ignore her symptoms, hoping they would go away.

For the next sixty minutes, they behaved like little kids let loose in a candy store. PLEASE TOUCH, a sign read at one of the tables laden with mostly chipped glassware and cracked crockery. Faith promptly took a picture of the sign, while Dana rummaged through the junk.

"I have a feeling there's a treasure to be found here," Dana muttered as she lifted up a heavy earthen bowl that had been mended in at least twenty places. "But this isn't it."

"A small breeze or one peanut would shatter it," Faith observed.

A shaggy-haired young man, his feet resting on the edge of a table, was reading a book, and studiously ignored the girls' comments.

Dana replaced the bowl on top of the crowded table and idly picked up a dish that was covered with dust. She blew off the dust, and gazed in amazement at the delicate pink porcelain decorated with tiny violet flowers.

"This is beautiful," she breathed.

"That's your treasure!" Faith exclaimed. "And there's a whole pile of them."

Dana counted ten dessert plates, and though smudged with dirt, they were in perfect condition.

"Excuse me, but how much are these?" Dana asked.

. The young man didn't respond, and Dana repeated her question. He still didn't give any signs of having heard her, and Dana moved closer to him, so close that she could see what he was reading.

"Emily Dickinson!" she cried out. "I don't believe it."

He looked at her quizzically. "Something wrong?"

"Why no, it's just that she happens to be my favorite poet and I didn't expect to see anyone reading poetry here. I mean. . . ." Dana's voice trailed off as she realized how awful she was sounding. But the truth was, she was shocked to see this rather scruffy-looking Midwesterner so totally absorbed in a collection of poetry at a trash and treasure sale.

"I like poetry," he said simply. "And since I have to sit here all day — as a favor to my mother — I might as well enjoy myself."

"Absolutely," Dana said, and beamed her dazzling smile at him.

Her smile was not without its effect, and the young man marked his place with a chewing gum wrapper, closed the book, and removed his feet from the table. "Anything I can help you with?" he asked. "I haven't made a sale all day."

"I think you're about to." Dana held up one of the plates. "How much are these?" she asked.

"Ten cents a piece."

"You're kidding!"

"Too much?"

"Too little."

"I'll charge more if it'll make you happy."

"It's okay, I'll settle."

They were both trying to be serious, but Faith, who was listening to the transaction, couldn't help laughing.

"My friend's a great bargainer," she said. "Maybe she could get the price up on this old Brownie camera."

"I'm sure I could," Dana assured her. "It's probably a collector's item."

"Is fifty cents enough?" he asked, somber-faced.

"Make it seventy-five and you have a sale," Faith said.

They were still laughing when Shelley spotted them and raced over to where the bargaining was taking place.

"What's so funny?" she demanded. "Are you taking advantage of my friends, Kenny?"

"Your friends — these are your friends? Might have guessed it, Shelley. They must be from the East."

"You guessed it," Shelley said, and explained who they were and that Kenny was a friend of Larry's, and that he wanted to teach English, and that they'd all meet later at the hayride.

Kenny wrapped up the plates in newspaper, and collected the money from the girls. Dana wanted to linger and talk about Emily Dickinson. "Don't you think she has a sense of humor, as well as. . . ."

"Not now," Shelley protested. "I want to show you these punk earrings that I saw at the jewelry booth. They're battery operated and light up."

"First things first," Dana said, smiling, and picked up the plates.

"This camera is a find. Can't wait to show it in my photography class."

"And I can't wait to give these plates to my mother. She'll love them," Dana said.

"And my mother will be so happy that I

made a sale," Kenny remarked indifferently. He resumed his reading position — chair tilted back, legs stretched out on the table — and picked up his book.

Kenny was already engrossed in his reading as Shelley urged her roommates to move. "Come on, gang, before somebody grabs up those earrings." She skipped ahead, while Dana and Faith slowly followed.

"That Kenny's not your typical small-towner — or is he?" Faith murmured under her breath to Dana.

"A shaggy cowboy who likes poetry doesn't seem typical. But who knows?" Dana mused. "This town is full of surprises."

CHAPTER EIGHT

"What do you do on a hayride? Just sit around and gaze at the stars?" Faith asked, flopping down on the daybed. She and Dana had come upstairs after supper to get ready.

"And sing songs, I suppose," Dana answered. She was standing in front of the mirror over the dresser, fixing her hair.

"I knew I should have brushed up on 'Old MacDonald Had a Farm' and 'Farmer in the Dell'," Faith said.

"Shelley says hayrides are a lot of fun," Dana remarked.

"If you want to ride around on a pile of straw with a bunch of people you don't even know. And it's so hot and muggy. . . ."

Dana stopped brushing her hair, and stared at her friend's reflection in the mirror.

"Hey, Faith, what's the matter?" she asked.

Faith sighed wearily. "I don't know," she

answered. "I guess I'm afraid I'll be the only black at the party."

"So what?" Dana scolded. "So far no one has treated you any different from the way they've treated me. We're both strangers in a strange land — nothing to do with being black or pink or polka-dotted."

Faith smiled wearily at the image. "Maybe I'm just tired." Faith knew she wasn't just tired. She was exhausted, and every move she made required an enormous effort. She was also scared that she had some awful disease but she wanted to hide her fear.

"You sound like you're ninety years old. Don't tell me you want to stay home?"

"Course not," Faith said, and pulled herself up.

"Then look alive. You act as though. . . ."

Just then Shelley popped into the room, her battery-operated earrings ablaze, one green and the other red. "Aren't they terrific?" she asked, pointing to her ears. "I'm glad you didn't talk me out of them."

"Unusual," Dana chuckled.

"They look like stop-and-go lights," Faith said.

"I never thought of that. If they're both on at once, I won't know whether I'm coming or going."

This brought on a case of giggles and Faith suddenly felt better. Whatever was bothering her magically disappeared and she thought how impossible it was to be around Shelley and not be in a good mood.

Shelley was going on about how you could give "yes" and "no" signals with such earrings and had Faith and Dana doubled over in laughter when a horn started honking persistently.

"Uh-oh. That's Jeff. I told him we'd be right down. He and Larry are waiting to drive us over." Shelley turned off her red earring and flashed the green, which broke them up again.

Then the girls grabbed their bags, Faith slung her camera around her neck, and they hurried downstairs.

"Where's Laurie?" Shelley asked Larry as she settled in the backseat of the station wagon.

"Had to go to her grandmother's sixtieth birthday party. And where's Paul?"

"I'm meeting him at the church."

"I thought this was a hayride, not a prayer meeting," Dana kidded.

"It's sponsored by the church. The Women's Auxiliary plans this every summer, and farmers lend their horses and wagons. A lot of my friends from junior high will be there and they're dying to meet you guys. It's going to be great!"

It took less than five minutes to arrive at the church, and Dana and Faith could see immediately that the atmosphere was charged with excitement. Paul was waiting impatiently for their arrival and ran up to them as soon as they hopped out of the wagon. He kissed each girl on the cheek, and then Shelley dragged Dana and Faith into the center of the crowd.

Shelley yelled with delight every time she met an old junior high school friend, and proudly showed off her roommates. Somewhat to Dana and Faith's embarrassment, she announced that they'd never been on a hayride before.

"It doesn't take much skill — all you have to be able to do is sit or lie down," said a cherubic-looking girl named Cary whom Shelley had described as her best Pine Bluff friend. "Nothing to worry about except getting straw in your hair."

Dana and Faith found themselves the center of attention, with everyone trying to make them feel at home. They'd both been afraid that they'd have to feel dependent on Shelley and Larry and Jeff — Faith especially was worried — but everyone was friendly. Jeff would have been no help at all in the beginning because he was immediately surrounded by a bunch of girls, all vying for his attention. At one point he caught Dana's eye and shrugged his shoulders as if to say, "What can I do?" Then he mouthed the words, "Help me."

There wasn't much time for Dana to do anything but smile at his predicament because a tall craggy-looking man, wearing a

weather-beaten Stetson, was urging everyone to pile on the wagon that was ready for
them behind the church.

"The Women's Auxiliary is expecting us
back at the church for refreshments, and we
don't want to be keeping them up too late.
Let's go!"

Everyone, more than thirty kids, rushed to
the back of the church where two horses
were hitched up to a wagon steeped with hay.
"Are we all going to fit on that?" Faith asked.

"That's what's fun," someone answered.
"Staying afloat is a challenge," said another.
"Haven't lost a hayrider yet," a third quipped.

Faith was embarrassed that she'd asked
such a dumb question, but she soon recovered
as she found herself being pulled onto the
wagon by the experienced kids who had
boosted themselves up unassisted. And she
joined in the laughter as she tried to disen-
tangle herself from a jumble of arms, legs,
and straw. But she felt limp as a cat, and
was glad that she could lie back and rest
without drawing any special attention to
herself.

"Everyone aboard?" the Stetson-hatted
man asked from his seat at the front of the
wagon.

"Don't see any strays, Clarence." It was
Kenny, who stood up next to him and peered
around. A paperback book was tucked under
his arm, and although it was still light, Dana
wondered when he'd find time to read.

"Hey, Clarence, can I hold the reins?" a pouty-looking girl with a squeaky voice asked.

"Soon as we get away from the downtown traffic, Dee Dee," Clarence answered.

"Traffic?" Dana muttered to Faith. "You'd have to be in the middle of the Sahara desert to find fewer cars than are here on a weekday evening in Pine Bluff."

There was a lot of whooping and shouting, and Dana and Faith expected a spectacular take-off. But it took several seconds for the wagon to budge, which everyone found hilarious. Then, amid cries of "Giddyap!" "Charge!" "Move it!" the wagon started up like molasses, gradually gathered momentum, and once it hit the paved road kept a slow but steady pace.

They had been traveling along less than five minutes when someone began singing and everyone joined in. They were immersed in the music and the high spirits, but Faith suffered a momentary longing for her boyfriend, Johnny, as she noticed Paul's arm around Shelley.

Johnny Bates was Faith's first serious boyfriend, and they'd been going together ever since he bumped into her with his ice-cream cone at the Tutti Frutti. Being in love with Johnny had made Faith's life at Canby Hall more fun than ever. He was everything she wanted — handsome, fun, but serious about wanting a career that would be of public service. His plan to join the police force with the hope of becoming a detective terrified her at first because her father had been killed in the force, but she finally came to terms with the idea.

She missed Johnny desperately at moments like this, when everyone else seemed to be part of a couple, but she knew their separation was temporary. Besides, the merriment was contagious, and she wouldn't let herself feel down. She closed her eyes and felt better as she fantasized about Johnny being beside her.

Meanwhile, Jeff had maneuvered himself close to Dana and put his arm around her shoulder. She snuggled against him and it seemed like the most natural thing in the world for him to tilt back her head and press his lips against hers. Dana didn't resist, and found herself kissing him back, but then she pulled away.

"What's wrong?" Jeff asked.

"Nothing . . . it's just that we hardly know each other." Dana knew that sounded idiotic, but she couldn't think of anything else to say.

"You're only going to be here a short time, and I really think you're special. I might not see you ever again." Jeff held her hand and looked deeply into her eyes.

"I really like you, Jeff, but. . . ." Dana floundered, not able to tell him the truth — that she was annoyed with herself for responding to him so easily. She didn't want to be casual about who she kissed, and in a very brief time there'd been Bret, then Randy, and now Jeff.

"If you really like me . . ." Jeff began.

But before he could finish his sentence the sky darkened dramatically, a bolt of lightning flashed, and a deafening clap of thunder drowned out his voice. Then it began to rain, drenching everything in sight, but the high spirits of the group were unquenchable and they shouted with delight at the unexpected downpour.

They had come to a slight incline and Clarence pulled the horses up short. "Keep going," someone insisted. "It's only a little rainstorm."

"It's more than that," Clarence said, trying to keep his voice steady. "It's a twister."

"He's right," Kenny shouted, and pointed towards a valley several hundred yards off the road where a funnel of air was moving.

Larry had scrambled towards Jeff, and murmured, "We better get out of here."

Dana sensed his anxiety, and asked in a low voice, "Are we in any real danger?"

"There's no telling which way it'll go," Larry answered.

"I'm scared," Dee Dee cried. "I want to go home."

"Me too," a boy with a surprisingly deep voice said.

A wave of panic swept across the crowd, voices rose to a hysterical pitch, and the fear was palpable.

One boy stood up in the middle of the wagon, nonsensically flailed his arms, and yelled, "I want to get out of here. We're all going to get killed."

Kenny deftly climbed over bodies to where he was standing, and told him sternly to sit down and be quiet. He looked glazed for a second, but then sank down on the straw, and remained still.

Clarence shouted, "I want everyone to stay calm. We've got to find shelter and I think the closest possible place is the abandoned barn on the old Campbell farm. It's hard to see, but my guess is it's about five hundred feet up on the right side of the road."

The crescendo of noise gradually diminished and was replaced by an eerie hush as Clarence urged the horses forward. Clarence, grateful that the hayriders were holding their tendency to hysteria in check, glanced around and said, "Someday you'll tell your grandchildren about the most exciting hayride you ever had!"

There were a few nervous giggles, but everyone was too scared to really laugh. Dana and Faith, along with the others, were mesmerized by the funnel that became blacker as it swirled through the valley, drawing in loose earth and debris.

"What can a twister do?" Dana asked Jeff, who looked unusually grim. She had instinctively curled up against him, grateful for the protection of his strong body and the feel of his comforting arm around her shoulder.

"I don't want to scare you," Jeff answered, "but it can uproot a tree, turn a telephone pole into a pretzel, toss a man hundreds of feet into the air, destroy a house. . . ."

"You're kidding!" Dana was incredulous, and pressed herself closer to him.

"Guess you never heard about the tornado in Waco, Texas, in '53," Larry said. "I thought everyone knew about that."

"Tell us," Faith said. Her concern about her health was momentarily overshadowed by imminent disaster.

"In ten minutes the tornado gouged a path a half mile wide and three miles long. It struck more than five hundred homes, killed eleven people, and seriously injured more than sixty."

Faith and Dana were speechless, and watched in terror as the funnel whirled along the ground. The idea that they could be swept up like rag dolls was terrifying. Strong young men like Larry and Jeff would be powerless against this freakish element of nature. The other hayriders were no longer able to contain their fright, and their noisy shouts intensified. The sky had darkened, but it was possible to follow the course of the twister.

"I'm scared," Dana muttered into Jeff's shoulder.

"This is just a baby twister," he tried to reassure her. "And it's about a half mile away."

"It's a big enough baby to fly us to the moon," Shelley said. She and Paul were huddled together.

At that moment, Clarence slowed the wagon and turned off the road. "We're here," he yelled. "This will provide some shelter till this thing blows over."

Everyone was relieved to have something to do besides sit passively, and they scurried into the front door of the barn. Clarence, with the help of a few older kids, coaxed the horses into the back door. Then everyone hovered around the entrance where they could see what was happening. There was one farm in the valley, and no one mentioned the unspeakable — the possibility that it might be destroyed.

All eyes peered in that direction, and then, as if on signal, there was a chorus of screams as the twister tore off the roof of the farmhouse in the valley. The hayriders gasped as they saw the roof hurtle into the air, shatter into a million pieces like a crushed match stick, and then fall to the ground.

Shelley, who was standing next to Faith and Dana, sobbed, "That's the Brown's farmhouse . . . they've got one little kid . . . what if they're. . . ."

She couldn't finish the thought as the funnel changed direction and zeroed in towards the barn where the hayriders were standing. Racing at thirty-five miles an hour, it would take only minutes to destroy the barn and everyone in it. Screams pierced the air, and Dee Dee shrieked out what everyone else knew: "It's coming our way!"

The noise reached a fever pitch, and the horses, sensing the danger, moved restlessly against their tethers. There was no place to escape from the turbulent black mass that zoomed relentlessly toward them.

"This is it," a voice said resignedly, and the shrillness intensified.

"We're finished," said another. There were whimpers and sobs, and even Clarence couldn't bring himself to say anything hopeful. Jeff and Dana held each other tight, neither of them able to speak.

Then, miraculously, the funnel slowly lifted, and the noise subsided as they watched it rise. Clarence let out a whoop of joy. "We're okay!" he roared. "We're okay!"

The black funnel rose higher and higher, and finally disappeared from sight. There was pandemonium in the barn — hugging and kissing and ear-splitting screams of relief and joy.

"Okay, gang," Clarence yelled above the crowd. "Quiet, please!"

He waited while everyone settled down, and then said, "You've behaved magnificently, but I have a feeling you'd like to get out of this barn and dry off before we all shrivel.

And if we don't lower the volume, the horses will be too skittish to move."

"Let's hear it for Clarence!" Kenny cried, and they all cheered.

A broad grin spread across Clarence's face, and when they quieted down he said, "I told you this would be one of the most exciting hayrides in history!"

Clarence brushed the back of his sleeve across his eyes, but since they were inside, it was clear that the drops that spilled down his face weren't from the rain, but from his relief.

Minutes later the horses were led out and harnessed to the wagon. Everyone leaped up, gleefully babbling about how scared they had been, kidding about how they were too young to die, wondering what their parents would say.

Faith had trouble climbing into the wagon and never would have made it if Larry hadn't seen her struggling and extended his hand to her. She joked about having been paralyzed with fear, and Larry fortunately didn't ask any questions. But the truth was that Faith's knees felt like jelly, and her head was pounding. This wasn't just an ordinary headache, caused by all the terror and excitement. Faith knew she was sick.

CHAPTER NINE

News of the twister spread through the town instantaneously, and the half dozen women who were preparing refreshments at the church had stayed glued to the radio, hanging onto every word of the local newscaster. They kept running to the window, but the dark clouds and heavy rain made it hard to see. It wasn't until the wagon pulled up to the door that one woman saw it and shouted, "They're safe! They're safe!"

The group was jubilant as it straggled into the church, and the women burst into tears of joy as they embraced the dripping wet hayriders. Everyone talked at once, telling about the flying roof and how the funnel had changed direction. They seemed indifferent to the fact that they were soaked to the bone, until Clarence made an announcement.

"I hate to throw cold water on you," he began, setting off a roar of laughter, "but we've just come through an ordeal, and I don't believe in tempting fate by having you risk pneumonia. We'll have to cut the party short and. . . ."

He was interrupted by a chorus of sighs and groans, but Clarence raised his voice and finished, "We'll continue it tomorrow morning at Neal's. He and his family are fine, but they need us."

"Where's Neal's?" Dana asked.

"Can't believe there's an all-night disco in Pine Bluff," Faith commented.

"Not exactly," Shelley said, smiling. "He's talking about Neal Brown's. That's whose roof we saw flying."

"And that's where the party is going to be?" Faith's eyes widened in amazement.

"Well, it's sort of a party. You see, whenever there's a disaster or someone's in trouble, everybody in town tries to help. As you saw with your very own eyes, the Browns no longer have a roof. So tomorrow all the people who are able to get away will help put up a new one. And since their kitchen is probably a shambles, people will bring over food for the family, who will probably spend the night with friends or relatives."

"That's wonderful," Dana said, and thought how in New York you could live next to the same neighbors for years and not even know their names.

On the way back to the house, Dana and Faith couldn't stop talking about how unusual it was for strangers to help each other out, but the Hydes kept insisting that no one in Pine Bluff was a stranger. "Even if we don't know them personally," Shelley said.

Shelley's parents had been waiting impatiently on the porch and flew down the steps when they saw the station wagon.

"I know you're fine," Mrs. Hyde cried as she and her husband took turns hugging the bedraggled arrivals.

"We called the church as soon as we saw the rainstorm," Mr. Hyde said. "Then we heard about the twister. . . ." His voice trailed off as he gave Shelley another quick hug, and it was obvious that he'd been more than a little anxious.

Everyone elaborated on the gory details with relish, now that they were safe.

"You kids better dry off," Mrs. Hyde advised.

"Girls first!" Shelley said, grabbing her roommates by the hand, and pulling them into the house.

"I'll be last," Faith volunteered when they arrived at the top of the stairs. "I feel like taking my time in the bathtub, and then I think I'll sack out."

"This wild Pine Bluff life *is* exhausting," Shelley teased. Then she turned to Dana. "Do you mind if I take the first shower? Paul said he'd drop by and I don't want to keep him waiting. He wants to go for a stroll —

says he hasn't been alone with me for ages."

"Go right ahead," Dana said. "I can see what he means. Besides, I hear your Mom playing the piano, and I'm in one of my listening moods."

By the time Dana came downstairs, Larry, Jeff, and Mr. Hyde were just going outside to assess the damage to the lawn, and Mrs. Hyde was absorbed in a medley of Gershwin tunes. Dana sank down on the comfortable chair near the piano, closed her eyes, and listened contentedly to the music. It was hard to believe that Mrs. Hyde hadn't studied piano for years, and when she finished, Dana asked her where she had learned to play.

"I had an older cousin who taught me the scales and chords when I was ten years old. Once I learned to read the notes, everything else came very naturally."

"But you're so good. Didn't you ever consider a career in music? I mean with all that talent, you must have been tempted."

"I was for a minute," Mrs. Hyde said, smiling. "I had a teacher in high school, a Mrs. MacGregor, who used me as an accompanist for the chorus. She forced me to play classical musicals. She was very encouraging about my ability — just like you, Dana."

"And she wanted you to study seriously?"

"That's right. She said I probably wouldn't have any difficulty getting a scholarship to the University of Indiana, which has a terrific music department. She would have written letters of recommendation, and since I had good marks, there wouldn't have been a problem."

"Then why didn't you?"

"I had to make a choice — between going to college and pursuing a career, or marrying Shelley's father."

"Couldn't you do both?"

"Not easily. You see, Bob was just starting out in the drugstore, and there was no way I could have commuted between Pine Bluff and Bloomington. I might have missed out on a big career, but I've never had a single moment's regret. Being a homemaker and raising a family has been the most gratifying kind of life for me."

"But don't you miss playing for an audience — besides your family?" Dana wondered if she could ever resist having a glamorous career if it was in easy reach, the way Mrs. Hyde's had been.

"I still occasionally have a recital in the church, and I'm involved in a lot of amateur theatrical productions in town. It's a lot of fun and gives me all the recognition I need."

Dana frowned thoughtfully. "But you wanted Shelley to go to Canby Hall. And now, because of her interest in acting, she might decide to go to Hollywood or head for Broadway, instead of returning to Pine Bluff and settling down. Doesn't that worry you?"

"No. I honestly believe that everyone should do their own thing, and although

Shelley's father and I have tried our best to give our kids good values, we don't want to dictate their lives. We've never pressured them to have a career to suit us. By sending them to college — and sending Shel to boarding school — they've learned there's life beyond Pine Bluff. I like to think I've given them options."

"That's wonderful." Dana thought what a remarkable woman Mrs. Hyde was . . . that in spite of her conviction about her own lifestyle being right for her, she saw that it might not be right for everyone, including her children.

"What about you, Dana. What do you want?"

"All I know for sure is that I want to be an architect . . . unless I become a famous poet," she said, laughing. "And like my mother, if I ever do get married and have kids, I'll probably be a working mother. My kid sister Maggie wants to be a juggler. Of course, she's only thirteen."

"Whatever you do, Dana, the important thing is to feel good about yourself. That's what I tell Shelley. She shouldn't decide to marry and settle down just to please me and her father. She's got to do what makes her happy."

"It's not always easy to know what that is."

"I know it isn't, but you'd be surprised how suddenly everything falls into place."

"If you're lucky," Dana said wistfully. "Only if you're lucky."

After Mrs. Hyde went upstairs to bed, Dana went out on the porch and sat down in the swing couch. The hot, muggy atmosphere had changed, and the night air was clear and fresh. Dana was happy to be alone for a while, to mull over her conversation with Shelley's mother. Mrs. Hyde had revealed a lot about herself, and Dana saw her in a new light. She wasn't just Shelley's mother — kind and loving — but a woman whose life could have gone in many directions. If Mrs. Hyde had decided to opt for a big career, she might have starred in a musical production on Broadway or the Kennedy Center, or even played at Carnegie Hall. If nothing else, Dana thought, the one thing she'd learned in the short time she'd been in Pine Bluff was that it was wrong to put people into categories.

At that moment Jeff appeared. He had changed into dry clothes, but his hair, still damp from the shower, framed his face and made him look more handsome than ever.

"Mind if I join you?" he asked.

In answer, Dana made room for him on the seat. It wasn't like Dana to be so quiet, and after several minutes Jeff asked her what she was thinking.

"I'm thinking that people aren't always what they seem."

"You'll never believe this, Dana, but I was thinking the same thing . . . about you, specifically."

"Meaning?"

"Meaning I thought you were so sophisticated and sure of yourself, but when that twister looked like it might do us in, you suddenly became very reachable."

"I was scared, Jeff, but you took it all in stride, like you were used to them."

"I'd never seen anything like it in all my eighteen years, but I figured it wouldn't do any good to panic no matter how hairy things got. And it did give me a chance to . . . to take care of you, if only for a minute." He smiled at her and added, "I think I'd be willing to risk all kinds of disasters if it meant holding you close again."

"That might not happen for another eighteen years, and I've only got ten days left." Dana grinned, surprised at her boldness, but she wasn't displeased when Jeff took the hint, encircled her with his arms, and kissed her lingeringly on the lips.

CHAPTER TEN

Shelley burst into Faith's and Dana's room early the next morning. "Gotta get up!" she said. "We have to go to the Brown's. My mom is already baking a ham for them."

Dana buried her head under the pillow, and Faith didn't budge.

"You don't understand, it's our civic duty — and also a lot of fun — to help out. Neal and his wife, Sally, just bought the farm and they haven't even paid for it yet. And Sally's expecting a baby any minute and they've got Abigail. . . ."

Dana muttered something unintelligible and Faith remained silent.

"I may have to resort to drastic means if you don't move immediately." Shelley spoke in a low, gruff voice. "The cold water treatment. . . ."

"Not that," Dana cried, "I'll do anything. . . ." and she threw off the pillow and bounded out of bed.

"One to go," Shelley said, and started to yank Faith's sheet off her bed.

"Leave me alone," Faith mumbled, her eyes still closed, and turned towards the wall. "I'm tired and I don't. . . ."

"No excuses," Shelley interrupted. "We have things to do, places to go, people to see!"

"Okay, okay," Faith said sleepily. Her eyes were half-closed as she groped on the floor for the glasses she wore when her contacts were out.

"Here." Shelley handed her her glasses which had been on the sewing table. "Now, I don't want to pressure you, but we should get rolling soon. We're on the first shift."

"What's that mean?" Dana asked, making her bed.

"I volunteered to take care of their three-year-old this morning. Abigail is really cute but she'll get in the way of the people who are going to fix the barn. Our plan was to have a picnic at the swimming hole, and I'll just bring her along. People will be drifting back and forth all day trying to help out."

"Sort of an open house," Dana surmised.

"More like an open roof," Shelley said, and then ducked out of the room before she got hit by the pillow Dana was ready to throw. She called back, "Don't forget your bathing suit. Best thing is to wear it as underwear."

* * *

It was a crystal clear day, which was often the case after a twister, Shelley explained as she drove Faith and Dana to the valley. She started to describe what happens. "A cold dry air mass moves in, and the warm air. . . ."

Faith had had two cups of black coffee but she was overcome with drowsiness and her head fell on Shelley's shoulder.

"Hey, I didn't mean to put you to sleep," Shelley said, gently nudging her.

"Huh?" Faith mumbled.

"Wake up," Dana said. "You're missing Shelley's meteorological lecture."

"That's right," Shelley confirmed. "You better listen, because I'm going to ask questions later."

Faith smiled and forced herself to stay awake while Shelley continued her explanation.

It was only ten o'clock when they arrived at the Brown's farm, but the place was bustling with activity. Jeff and Larry were among the men who were cutting lumber to size for a new roof, and they waved to the girls as they got out of the car. In the kitchen women from the community — many were familiar faces from the women's auxiliary — were preparing enough dishes for a banquet. Dana and Faith were treated like old friends as they helped Shelley bring in the ham. Abigail, as predicted, was underfoot.

Sally kissed Shelley and cried, "I couldn't wait till you got here."

"These are my friends, Dana and Faith. What can we do?"

"The best thing will be to get Abby out of here," Sally said laughing. "And I think it'll take three of you to handle her."

"We'll take her to the swimming hole with us. We were going to have a picnic there, anyways."

"Terrific. I'll get her suited up with water wings," Sally said, and whisked Abigail away from the oven where she looked like she was about to crawl in with the cookies that were being baked.

Jeff had come into the kitchen for a glass of water. "I'll meet you at the swimming hole at noon. Mr. Jensen doesn't expect me back till this afternoon, and he wouldn't want me to go without lunch."

"Course not," Shelley said. "Mom made a pile of sandwiches for us. There's plenty."

Then the girls headed for the swimming hole which was less than five hundred feet away, with Abigail happily trotting to keep up with them. Shelley and Dana shed their clothes down to their bathing suits and jumped into the water, followed by Abigail who fearlessly splashed her way towards Shelley's open arms.

Faith, meanwhile, had settled under a tree, her legs stretched out and her head resting against the trunk.

"You look like you're planted there," Dana remarked. "Come on in."

"Later," Faith said, taking off her glasses and closing her eyes.

"You forgot your contacts," Shelley observed, and didn't wait for a reply as she ducked under the water so that Abigail could climb on her shoulders.

Abigail took turns playing "horsey" with Shelley and Dana until all three were exhausted. Then they climbed out, dried off with their towels, and persuaded Abigail to take a sunbath.

"Aren't you going in, Faith?" Dana asked idly, as she stretched out on a towel.

"Just don't feel like it now," Faith replied.

"You don't know what you're missing," Shelley said, raking her hair with a comb. Then she got busy straightening out Abigail's towel so that she could lie down.

"You don't feel well, do you?" Dana asked Faith in a low voice, propping herself up on one elbow and looking closely at her friend.

"I have a little headache, that's all," Faith answered.

"Maybe you should see a doctor."

"A doctor — in Pine Bluff? Don't be ridiculous. They probably have great veterinarians here, but since I don't have hoof-and-mouth disease, I think I'll scratch that idea."

"Can't say that I blame you." Dana was reassured by Faith's reaction.

"Besides, it might be I need new lenses. Haven't had my eyes checked since last fall."

"Probably that's it." Dana turned over and

concentrated on getting her back tan.

Abigail dozed off and the girls enjoyed the silence for almost five minutes, but their rest was cut short by what sounded like a stampede of wild animals.

The girls leaped up, momentarily alarmed, but relaxed when they saw that the pack of animals was actually a bunch of the Brown's helpers, headed by Jeff. They hallooed at the top of their lungs, and then plunged into the swimming hole. Then Jeff and Cary made themselves self-appointed captains and chose up teams for a frisbee water match. Shelley and Dana joined the others gleefully, but Faith refused. "I'll keep an eye on Abigail," she hedged. She put on her glasses and moved to the edge of the swimming hole where Abigail was sitting.

The frisbee zoomed back and forth, but after fifteen minutes of trying to stay afloat, with the passes getting weaker, and the players more breathless, the group mutually agreed that the game was a tie and they had to get back to work.

Only Jeff and a few others remained, and then Paul magically appeared while Shelley was distributing the sandwiches.

"Your timing is perfect," Shelley joked. "The roof's almost done and we're just about to have lunch."

"I'm on the afternoon shift, Shel. You knew that. I had to help my father out on a paint job this morning."

"Only kidding, Paul."

"You're learning to be such a good actress at Canby Hall that you had me fooled. Will the real Michelle Hyde please come forth!"

Paul's sarcasm wasn't lost on Shelley and a frown clouded her usually cheerful expression. They had agreed not to talk about Shelley's possible career in acting, which would mean she would undoubtedly move away from Pine Bluff, but Paul couldn't resist a few digs. He still resented the fact that Shelley had gotten involved with Tom who had acted in the school play with her. Their mutual interest in each other extended far beyond the theater. And what made matters worse, Paul had met Tom and thought he was a nice guy. It would have been easier for Paul if he'd regarded Tom as a wimp.

Shelley knew Canby Hall had changed her life — "broaden one's horizons" Miss Allardyce, the headmistress, had urged in one of her assembly talks. Shelley was usually half asleep during those early morning assemblies, but she had done exactly that. There was a huge world beyond Pine Bluff, and Canby Hall had made her aware of it. When she confided her feelings to Paul, he admitted she had every right to enjoy new experiences, but the idea of losing Shelley was sometimes more than he could take.

It was impossible for the others not to pick up on the by-play between Shelley and Paul. The tension eased slightly when Dana remarked, "These sandwiches are terrific."

"I could use one," Paul said, sitting on a flat rock, a little away from the others. "What have you got to offer?"

Shelley knew Paul regretted airing their personal problems and she didn't want to make him suffer. She carried the picnic basket over to him, stood like a waitress taking an order, and recited:

"Our specialties today are peanut butter and bacon, sliced turkey, ham and —"

"Ham, that's it!" he interrupted.

"Ham, I didn't know you liked ham."

"And you're my favorite," Paul said smiling, and pulled her down beside him.

"Oh, ham . . . actor . . . I get it!" Shelley laughed, and the others applauded with delight at the happy ending of the unrehearsed scene.

Later that night when Dana and Faith were alone in their room getting ready for bed, they talked about boys, bemoaned the fact that they were a constant source of worry, and wondered what they would do without them.

"Doesn't matter whether it's Pine Bluff or the Big Apple," Dana mused as she pulled a nightshirt over her head. "Boys can drive us crazy."

"And vice versa," Faith said. "I think if it weren't so close to showtime for Gerty, Jeff would quit his job and just hang out with you."

Dana shrugged her shoulders and smiled. "Maybe you're right. And if it were up to Paul, Shelley would give up Canby Hall and acting, and decide to be his wife. That scene at the swimming hole got a little tense, but fortunately they each have a sense of humor."

"Doesn't mean their problem is solved — just put on hold for a while. The same way I feel about Johnny. I mean I love him, but I still worry about his being a cop. One minute I think he's so wonderful for wanting to dedicate himself to helping others — solving crimes, protecting people — just like my father did before he was killed in a hold-up. But then I wonder if it's worth the risk."

Dana said softly, "I never thought my parents would split. I like my father's wife, Eve, but I miss having a whole family. My mother must, too, though she never talks about it. Do you think you can ever be absolutely sure about whether you're marrying the right person?"

The only sound from Faith was a steady zzzzzzzzzz. She was already fast asleep, and Dana knew there wasn't an answer to her question anyway.

Dana climbed into bed, her head buzzing with a zillion ideas. She still felt like talking and wished that Faith had stayed awake. She was even tempted to throw a slipper at her so that they could continue their conversation, but Faith had conked out so quickly that Dana thought it would be cruel to disturb her. Then she thought how lethargic Faith had been all day — falling asleep in the car, not wanting to go swimming. It wasn't like Faith to be so laid back. But then Dana decided maybe she acted that way because she missed Johnny so much. Shelley had Paul, she had Jeff, and Faith — at least for this vacation — had no one. *That's probably the problem,* Dana thought, as she drifted off to sleep.

It was less than twenty minutes later that Faith awoke with a start. The room was swimming and her head was pounding. She took several deep breaths before forcing herself to sit up. That position made her less dizzy, and she slowly swung her feet out of the bed. Her legs felt like liquid, but she hoped they would propel her down the hall to the bathroom.

She crept quietly out of the room, not wanting to disturb Dana, and stayed close to the wall. By stopping every few feet to rest, she finally made it to the sink where she gulped down an aspirin and a glass of water. She made the return trip cautiously, grateful that everyone's door was closed, and collapsed on the bed.

She entertained the idea of awakening Dana to tell her she was scared. Faith had had her share of childhood diseases —

measles, chicken pox, and a bout with scarlet
fever — but she'd never had a headache like
this. Maybe something was terribly wrong.
She was afraid to face that idea, and decided
that when the aspirin took effect, she'd feel
better. There was no point in telling Dana,
who would feel compelled to wake up Shelley,
who would probably insist on telling the rest
of the family. Soon everyone would be
alarmed.

Faith tossed and turned restlessly for half
the night and it was almost dawn before she
fell into a druglike sleep. When Dana awakened the next morning, she glanced at Faith
and thought whatever was bothering her
must certainly have been taken care of by
ten hours sleep!

CHAPTER ELEVEN

Friday
Midnight

Dear Maggie,

Here's the letter I promised. I can't believe less than a week has passed since I left home, so much has happened. For starters, I learned to ride Western and went on a hayride. It's been a whirlwind vacation, almost literally, because one night we barely escaped getting caught in a twister. I'll tell you the details when I get home. Anyhow, the result was that the roof of a nearby barn was blown off, and for the past couple days we've been helping out the family. But all this is tame compared to what's happening tomorrow. It's county fair day, which in Pine Bluff is like Christmas, Easter, Thanksgiving, Halloween, and any other holiday you can think of wrapped in one.

Jeff, who is Shelley's eighteen-year-old brother and really cute — looks just like a six-foot, blond, blue-eyed cowboy should — is showing his heifer, Gertrude, in the livestock exhibition. You'd think she was entering the Miss America contest the way everyone around here talks about her. But the excitement's contagious and I'm just as worked up as everyone else about whether she'll win a blue ribbon.

I have to run now. Shel is yelling at me to help her decide what to wear to the square dance that takes place in the school gym after the fair. It'll be a fantastic celebration if Gertrude wins. I hate to think about the bomb it'll be if she loses. Can you believe I'd get so involved with a cow?

The Hydes are super, but I miss you and Mom a lot.

Loads of love,
Dana

The next morning Dana awakened early and quickly got dressed. There wasn't much she could do to help Jeff, except give him moral support, but she wanted to see him before he left for the farm. She knew he would be leaving at the crack of dawn with Larry, who was going to help load Gertrude on Mr. Jensen's truck. The entire Hyde family was already downstairs, in various stages of having breakfast, when Dana entered the kitchen.

"Where's Faith?" Shelley asked, handing Dana a glass of freshly squeezed orange juice.

"Didn't have the heart to wake her, she was sleeping so soundly."

"We'll get to her later," Shelley said ominously.

"Jeff, don't eat so fast," Mrs. Hyde cautioned her son as he stood over the kitchen table, bolting down a bowl of cereal topped with bananas.

"I'm in a hurry, Mom," he gulped, shoving the last spoonful down. "Only four hours till countdown." Then he threw his arms around his mother, who smiled helplessly.

Mr. Hyde, who'd been sitting on the kitchen stool drinking his coffee, stood up and firmly shook Jeff's hand. "Good luck, son," he said.

"Break a leg, as they say in show biz," Shelley exclaimed, and pounded her brother affectionately on the back.

Then Jeff looked at Dana, who surprised herself by impulsively kissing him on the cheek. "Good luck," she whispered in his ear.

Jeff blushed, grasped her hands, and squeezed them tightly, hoping to communicate the depth of his feeling.

"Thanks, everyone." Jeff grinned shyly, hoping his face didn't look as red as it felt, and turned to his brother. "We've got to go now."

"Right," Larry said, getting up from the kitchen table where he'd been devouring three eggs and a rasher of bacon. "I'm stoked up now and ready to cope."

"We'll be getting to the fairgrounds around eleven," Mrs. Hyde told the boys as she pulled her pies out of the oven. "I have to deliver my pies, and the girls will want to wander around the other booths until it's time for the livestock show."

"You know where to find me," Jeff said. He headed for the door and held up his hands with his fingers crossed.

Dana and Shelley finished eating breakfast, and helped with the dishes. Then they trudged upstairs, discussing the best way to wake up Faith.

"Blasting music close to the ear always works," Shelley said.

"I personally think tickling the soles of the feet with a feather is most effective," Dana offered.

"What about just plain pulling the body out of the bed and onto the floor?"

But they didn't need to resort to any of these methods, because Faith was already dressed. She was bent over the edge of the bed, tying her sneakers, when the girls came into the room.

"Good girl!" Shelley exclaimed.

"You've been spared the unthinkable," Dana added.

Faith smiled wanly, stood up, and said, "I could use some coffee."

"There's still some in the pot, and we left out the cereal and bananas for you," Shelley said. "Now I've got to clean up my room." She went out, and Dana got busy putting her clothes away so that neither of them noticed how slowly Faith walked out of the room. Then Shelley called Dana in to help her make a final decision on what top to wear to the square dance that night. They boiled the decision down to two — a bright green and a lemon yellow — and Shelley was still debating which to choose when Faith appeared silently on the threshold.

"You look like a ghost," Shelley exclaimed as she saw Faith framed in the doorway.

"That will be the day," Faith muttered, a small grin briefly brightening her face. "But to tell the truth, I'm feeling a little ghostly."

"You feel sick?" Dana asked.

"You're not going to miss the fair, I hope," Shelley said.

"I hate to miss it, but I think I'm getting something. Probably just a cold, but I won't be much fun." Faith looked forlorn as she sank down on Shelley's bed.

"Maybe you'll feel better when you get some air. It's a beautiful day," Dana commented.

Just then Mrs. Hyde called from downstairs. "We're leaving in ten minutes, girls."

"We're ready, Mom," Shelley shouted. Then

she turned to Faith. "Are you sure you don't want to come?"

"I'm afraid I'll be a drag, but please don't make a big deal about it. I'll get some sleep and I'll probably be fine for the square dance."

"If you say so," Shelley conceded.

"And don't scare your mother. I don't want her to worry about me."

"That's not easy," Shelley mumbled.

"Maybe if you go downstairs and tell her yourself, she won't be so alarmed," Dana suggested.

"Good idea. If she sees I'm okay she won't be upset."

Just then Mrs. Hyde was passing by Shelley's door, muttering something about bringing her book in case there was a long wait before Gertrude was shown. She peeked in the room and said, "Dad's already in the car. I thought you were ready."

"We are, but Faith thinks she's getting a cold or something, and wants to stay home this morning," Shelley told her.

"Faith, honey, are you sure it's not serious?" Mrs. Hyde quickly walked over to where Faith was sitting on the bed and pressed the back of her hand against her forehead.

"I'm sure."

"You don't seem to be feverish, but do you mind being left alone?"

"Not at all. I'll take it easy and then I'll be in shape for the square dance tonight."

"But I could stay with you. . . ."

"Please, Mrs. Hyde," Faith pleaded, "I'll feel a zillion times worse if you don't go. I'm just going to sleep, anyways."

"She means it, Mom," Shelley said. "Otherwise I'd stay. Faith can be very stubborn."

"That's for sure," Dana confirmed.

"I guess I'm outnumbered," Mrs. Hyde said, and turned to leave. Then she looked back at Faith, and spoke in a serious voice. "Promise me you'll get some sleep."

"I promise," Faith said, and added with false gaiety, "I sure don't want to miss the dance."

But the minute they left, Faith let down her defenses and the tears spilled down her face. She couldn't understand what was happening to her physically, and she'd never felt so alone or afraid.

When they arrived at the fairgrounds, Shelley's parents promised to meet the girls after delivering the pies to the bakery booth. Shelley and Dana headed directly for the livestock exhibit, and had no trouble finding Gertrude's stall. Jeff was working on her tail, while Larry was feeding her beet pulp, and Mr. Jensen muttered words of advice.

"Comb the hair up, if you want to give the tail a fluffy appearance," he said.

It was hard for Dana and Shelley not to

smile at this crusty farmer offering beauty tips.

"Why don't you try hair spray?" Shelley asked.

For an answer, Jeff rummaged through a bag of equipment and came up with a spray can that had a label "For Hard-to-Hold Hair." He proceeded to use it on Gertrude's tail.

The girls cracked up, but Mr. Jensen explained evenly, "That's standard equipment for show animals."

"And it works," Dana observed.

Jeff smiled at Dana appreciatively. "Sure glad you got here, but where are my folks and what happened to Faith?"

"Mom and Dad are entering the pies in the contest. They'll be here soon."

"And Faith?"

"She didn't feel well. Thinks she's coming down with a cold."

"I don't believe it. A little cold would keep her away from the county fair? She'll never have the opportunity to see me show Gertrude again."

"She really wanted to come," Dana defended her friend.

"She figures if she takes it easy this morning, she'll be okay for the dance," Shelley said.

"The dance? Who cares about that?" Jeff, who had been under a lot of stress, was burning with anger. He started to say something else, but just then the Hydes appeared.

They greeted Mr. Jensen, and then Mrs. Hyde began emoting about Gertrude as though she were dressed for the junior prom. "I just know she'll walk off with a ribbon. I can't wait till she gets in that ring. . . ."

" 'Fraid you'll have to, Mom. The heifer class doesn't begin for two more hours."

"Lucky I brought my book."

"And I remembered to bring some pharmaceutical journals. Give me a chance to catch up on my reading," Mr. Hyde said.

"And I'll have more time to groom Gerty." Jeff was about to pour mineral oil on a flannel cloth.

"It's too early for that, Jeff," Mr. Jensen said. "You should apply oil to her coat for a gloss just before she goes in the ring."

"I want to keep busy," Jeff grumbled.

"Two hours is a long time, Jeff, and you're already sweating up a storm. Why don't you go home, take a shower, change clothes, and be back a half hour before showtime. Larry and I will keep an eye on Gerty."

Shelley and Dana looked at Mr. Jensen in astonishment. It was the longest speech they'd ever heard him make. And its impact wasn't lost on Jeff.

"Gee, that's a good idea. I do need to cool off. Okay with you, Larry?"

"Why not?" Larry answered. "This is a once-in-a-lifetime opportunity, and we've arranged to have the store covered."

"Let's all meet back here at two," Shelley

said. "That'll give Dana and me almost enough time to check out the booths, ride the ferris wheel, and sample some of the baked goodies. . . ."

"Just remember," Mr. Jensen cautioned Jeff, "the entrants must show the animal — no substitutions allowed — so be back here on time. You didn't groom Gertrude all this summer to have her miss her big moment."

"Tell me about it," Jeff said, and smiled at Mr. Jensen. For the moment, at least, he didn't seem quite so mad, and he hurried off.

Jeff forced himself not to speed on the way home. There was plenty of time, and he knew that hanging around Gertrude was making him nervous, and it probably wasn't doing her any good either. But he couldn't stop worrying about whether she would perform well and reviewed in his mind all the pluses and minuses.

Making sure she looked "dairy" perfect was his responsibility, and Jeff was convinced she was endowed by nature with the physical attributes worthy of a winner. However, she could be quite perverse when it came to responding to the lead.

Jeff gripped the steering wheel harder, and all his anxieties returned. Although it was unreasonable, he focused his anger on Faith.

A little cold shouldn't keep her away, he thought, his irritation increasing. *I think I'll tell her what a snob she is, afraid of a little*

fresh air because she sneezed twice. Or maybe
people from Washington, D.C. don't realize
how important the fair is in our lives. . . .

By the time Jeff pulled into the driveway
of the house, he was seething with rage. And
when he walked in the back door, he shouted,
"Where the heck are you? It wouldn't kill
you to come to the fair for a couple of hours!"

There was no answer, and Jeff was angrier
than ever as he bounded up the stairs and
stormed into his room. "She's not even here,"
he barked as he whipped off his clothes and
headed for the bathroom. "Probably clicking
away with her camera somewhere now that
there's no one around to interfere."

Jeff tried to relax as he turned the shower
spigot on full force, soaped up, and let the
water stream down. He rinsed off under a
blast of cold water, and although he felt
better physically as he dried off, he couldn't
stop muttering to himself about Faith's sel-
fishness.

"She feels well enough to leave the house,
but not to see Gertrude in her big moment.
How self-centered can you be?"

He put on some fresh clothes, still grum-
bling. Then he carefully combed his hair,
thinking he should look as neat as Gertrude,
and in order to kill time straightened up his
room. There were about thirty minutes left
until he should head back for the fair, so he
decided to wend his way downstairs and
have a Coke.

He ambled slowly down the hall, past the bathroom, past the sewing room. . . . For a second he thought he was hearing things. A sound was coming through the closed door and Jeff froze. *Probably Ginger, who managed to get herself locked in, or maybe Freckles.* . . . As a reflex action, having been trained to never barge into a room without knocking, he rapped on the door.

"Come in," a weak voice murmured.

Jeff opened the door slowly and was shocked to see Faith, fully clothed, sprawled on the bed. She was breathing heavily, beads of perspiration covered her lip, and her eyes were half closed.

"Oh, no!" Jeff cried, as he rushed to her side, his heart pounding, stricken with guilt and fear. "Faith, what happened?"

"Don't know," Faith breathed, and made a futile effort to sit up.

Jeff pressed his palm against her head, and quickly pulled it away as though he'd been stung. "You're burning up," he said. "Are you in pain? Where does it hurt?"

"All over," Faith answered, and tried hard to smile as though she were joking.

"I can't leave you like this."

"Please, Jeff, you've got to go back to the fair. I'll make it through the day." Faith was determined to make light of her illness, even though her head was killing her.

Jeff couldn't help thinking of Gertie, and how much time and energy he'd invested in

her. It would all go down the drain if he
didn't show up at the fair. And Faith was
urging him to leave. But Faith was sick,
maybe desperately, and she needed him.

"You're sick, Faith. I can't leave you," he
repeated, and saw clearly what he had to do.
"I've got to get you to County Hospital."

"Jeff, I'll be okay. Go. . . ." Faith spoke in
a whisper.

"No way," he said sternly, realizing she was
putting up a brave front.

"But what about Gerty?" Faith sobbed.
Her eyes filled with tears.

"There's always next year," Jeff told her.
"She'll be around." He pulled a clean handkerchief out of his pocket and blotted her
face.

"I feel awful," she sniffled.

"I know you do. That's why I'm taking you
to the hospital."

"That's not what I mean. I mean awful
because of all the trouble I'm causing."

Jeff ignored that and said, "We've got to
get you downstairs and then I can carry you."

"But Jeff, I don't want you to miss. . . ."

"Do what I say," Jeff insisted, and gently
pulled her to a sitting position. "Put your
arm around my neck and lean on me."

Faith was too weak to argue and limply
wrapped her arm around him. Then Jeff stood
up, holding her firmly by the waist. They
inched their way down the hall and slowly
negotiated the stairs.

"I better leave a note," Jeff said, and eased Faith into a chair just inside the living room.

Then he rushed into the kitchen, grabbed a pad and pencil, and hastily scribbled a note. *Faith sick. We've gone to the hospital.* He left it on the table in the vestibule, and hurried back to Faith who was slumped over, her head almost touching the floor.

"My head aches. . . . It's killing me," she whimpered. "And my throat. . . ."

Jeff was more alarmed than ever, for he realized that in the short time since he'd discovered Faith in her room, she had taken a turn for the worse. She was sweating all over, and at the same time she was shivering with chills.

"Don't worry. I'll get you to the hospital in ten minutes. It's in the next town, but I know exactly how to get there."

He lifted her in his arms, saw that she was practically unconscious, and raced out of the house. "I'll get you there, I'll get you there," he kept repeating as he leaned her against the side of the car and opened the door next to the driver's seat. He maneuvered her inside and rushed to the other side. The wheels screeched as he backed out of the driveway.

Jeff kept talking to Faith as he burned up the road, telling her everything would be all right. But he knew he was really reassuring himself because Faith was totally out of it. The traffic was unusually light, probably because everyone from the county was at the fair. Jeff had a pang of anguish as he thought about Gertrude, how worried his family must be, Mr. Jensen's disappointment. But his main concern was to get help for Faith, and everything else seemed unimportant.

The hospital was a small brick building and Jeff drove up to the side entrance marked Emergency. An attendant opened the door on the passenger side and immediately summed up the situation.

"You stay here. I'll get a stretcher," he said. He was a middle-aged man who had a pronounced limp, but he moved with amazing speed.

"Thanks," Jeff called after him, and sighed with relief as he watched him hurry inside.

Minutes later he returned with a muscular young man who pushed a stretcher with rollers towards the car. Then the two men skillfully lifted Faith onto the stretcher.

"Pull your car up and check in at the desk. We'll take care of the patient," the attendant instructed.

Jeff moved the car away from the entrance and then hurried to catch up with the stretcher which was being wheeled into a room off the center corridor.

"Hold it," a bantamlike woman sitting behind the reception desk barked at Jeff. "You're not allowed in there, and you have to give me some information."

"Oh, I do?" Jeff stopped short and spun around, obviously flustered.

The woman saw Jeff's concern and her manner softened. "Don't worry, your friend will get excellent care. Dr. Staunton's the resident physician on duty, and he's the best."

"Lewis Staunton, I've heard of him," Jeff said, and recalled his father mentioning that Dr. Staunton had an excellent reputation as a diagnostician and internist.

"Now, can you answer some questions?"

"I'll try," Jeff replied, and told as much about Faith as he could, explaining that she was visiting for two weeks, lived in Washington, D.C., and that there hadn't been time to notify her family. "What happens next?"

"The intern in charge of the emergency room will make a preliminary examination, and then he'll probably want to talk to you. You can wait over there." She pointed to a sofa and chairs grouped around a table piled with magazines.

"Thank you, Miss Gladstone," Jeff said, reading the identification card pinned to her jacket.

He went over to the sofa, sat down, and picked up a copy of *People*, but he couldn't get through one paragraph without glancing up, hoping the doctor would appear. Finally the intern did come out of Faith's room, strode purposefully toward the reception desk, and spoke to Miss Gladstone. Seconds later an announcement blared over the loudspeakers: *Dr. Staunton wanted in Emergency.*

Then Miss Gladstone pointed to Jeff, and the intern walked over to where he was sitting, introduced himself as Dr. Gabriel, and shook Jeff's hand.

"Do you know what's wrong?" Jeff asked, after telling who he was and how he'd rushed over to the hospital.

"Not yet. She has a high fever and chills, and is barely conscious. Has she complained about headaches?"

"Just before we came here, she said her head was killing her. Do you think she's very sick?"

"We won't know anything before we make some tests, and Dr. Staunton sees her. But I'd be kidding you — and myself — if I pretended she wasn't seriously ill."

Just then a short, bald-headed man in a white jacket, wearing wire-framed glasses, came off the elevator opposite the reception desk. He nodded briefly at Dr. Gabriel and went directly into Faith's room.

"That's Dr. Staunton," the intern said. "I'll let you know what's happening."

Jeff watched him until he was out of sight, and then stood up. He was no longer able to sit still, and he paced up and down the corridor. The intern's words were frightening and he couldn't get them out of his mind: *I'd be kidding you — and myself — if I pretended she wasn't seriously ill.*

CHAPTER TWELVE

Jeff went outside and looked up the road in the direction of Pine Bluff. It was after two and he hoped his family and Dana would be arriving soon. Thank goodness, he thought, that he'd had the brains to leave a note. At least they'd be assured that he hadn't totaled himself and the car, which would be the most logical explanation for him not to show up.

Jeff had never known the time to drag so slowly. He tried to distract himself by wandering back into the hospital and watching the real life dramas that were being enacted. A boy about eight years old was expertly using his crutches while his smiling parents checked him out at the reception desk.

"Don't do any tree-climbing for a while, Tommy," Miss Gladstone called to him as he went out the door.

Minutes later a distraught mother brought in a whimpering baby. The mother spoke

143

briefly to Miss Gladstone, who directed her
to one of the emergency rooms.

Then Jeff saw a nurse and an attendant
wheeling Faith into the corridor. There was a
bottle of fluid suspended from a thin pole
attached to the stretcher. The fluid was
dripping through a tube into a needle con-
nected to Faith's arm. Jeff knew this paraphernalia was for intravenous feeding, but
he'd only seen it used in movies or the soaps.
The sight of it being applied to Faith threw
him, and he tore over to her. Faith's eyes
were closed and she was breathing heavily.

"Is she okay?" Jeff asked the crisp-looking
nurse. He had trouble keeping his voice
steady.

"I can't answer that," she replied, not un-
kindly.

"Where you taking her?"

"To room 305."

"Can I go with you?"

"The doctor's ordered no visitors until he
has the results of some tests."

"Why all that intravenous stuff?"

"To provide nutrients."

"But can't she. . . ."

Jeff started to ask more, but the elevator
had arrived. "Later," the nurse said, looking
relieved that she could avoid answering
further questions. Then she efficiently helped
the attendant roll the stretcher into the
elevator. Jeff watched as the door closed, and
he could feel his heart sink. He'd never felt so

helpless and he walked around the corridors aimlessly, hoping that someone would tell him everything was all right. But what if it wasn't? What if Faith. . . . ? He couldn't bear to finish the thought, and continued pacing up and down.

Finally the Hydes and Dana arrived, and Mrs. Hyde, seeing how distraught Jeff was, silently embraced him. But Shelley couldn't restrain herself from asking him what was uppermost on everyone's mind. "Is Faith going to be all right? Where is she? Has the doctor seen her?"

Several people were milling around the reception desk, and they stared curiously at Shelley, who couldn't hide her anguish.

"Why don't we move over here," Mr. Hyde advised calmly, and led the way to an empty corner of the floor where there was a bench and some chairs.

"Please, Jeff, tell us what you know," Dana pleaded, as they sat down.

"Not much, I'm afraid," Jeff said, and then described everything that had happened from the time he'd found Faith until he saw her being wheeled into the elevator.

"Let's go see her," Shelley exclaimed, jumping up. "You say she's in room 305."

"No visitors, Slugger. You heard Jeff," Larry said.

"Not even me and Dana? We're her best friends."

"We have to do what the doctor says," Mr.

Hyde told her. "And Dr. Staunton is one of the most respected medical men in the Midwest."

"We're fortunate he's on the staff," Mrs. Hyde concurred. "And I am going to try and talk to him. I want to get more information so that when we call Faith's mother tonight she'll know the situation."

"I'll go with you, honey." Mr. Hyde stood up and grasped his wife's hand. Then, just before he walked off, he turned to Jeff. "You made some very tough decisions today, Jeff, and we're very proud of you."

"Jensen figured you had to be struck with the bubonic plague to keep you away," Larry added.

Dana half-smiled at Jeff, who she knew was ready to go through the floor if he received one more compliment. But she couldn't help saying, "You may have saved Faith's life."

Silence fell like a veil over the usually exuberant group. Dana and Shelley looked at each other and their eyes filled with tears. Jeff's shoulders drooped and his head hung down, a picture of total exhaustion.

Larry looked at his brother and said, "I think you could stand a cup of coffee. There's a snack bar downstairs, and you probably haven't had a chance to have lunch."

"I did forget about food," Jeff said wearily. "And that does sound like a good idea."

"Can we bring you anything?" Larry asked

the girls as he and Jeff started to leave.

They shook their heads and watched the boys head for the elevator. Shelley instinctively moved closer to Dana on the bench, threw her arms around her, and then they both dissolved in tears.

"I can't believe this is happening," Shelley sobbed, and fumbled in her pocket for some tissues. She handed a couple to Dana, and the girls blew their noses, wiped their eyes, and tried to pull themselves together.

"It's my fault," Dana murmured, once she had regained her composure. "I feel so guilty."

"Your fault? That's crazy!" Shelley protested. "You didn't make her sick."

"She's been feeling crummy ever since we arrived, but I didn't do anything about it. If I hadn't been so self-involved. . . ."

"If anything, I should take the blame for Faith getting sick. I was so afraid of not keeping you guys busy, that I planned too many things. I wanted so much for you to love it here. . . . It's all my fault." Shelley's voice broke and tears welled up in her eyes again.

"But we did have a great time . . . until now. And if I'd only listened to Faith, or noticed some of the symptoms, maybe this could have been avoided."

"Like what? I can't remember anything. . . ."

"She complained of being dizzy the day we

went riding, and she acted so tired before the hayride, and afterwards she said her head ached. She's been sleeping an awful lot, too."

"Now that you mention it, she was really out of it the day we went swimming. She wouldn't even get her feet wet."

"That's right. And she told me then that she had a headache, but that it was probably because she needed new lenses. . . . Oh, Shel, how could I be so dense?"

"Me, too," Shelley sighed. "She must have felt awful all along, and the only thing I noticed was that she wasn't wearing her contacts." Shelley began to cry again, and Dana gently patted her shoulder.

"Look, Shel, this isn't doing either of us any good, and it sure isn't helping Faith."

"You're right, Dana. We've got to be optimistic and we sure don't want Faith to see us with our chins in our boots — whenever we do get to see her." They straightened up then, just as Shelley's parents and brothers approached from opposite directions.

Mr. and Mrs. Hyde sat down heavily in the chairs facing Shelley and Dana. Mrs. Hyde looked grim.

"Is the news bad?" Shelley asked.

"Dr. Staunton doesn't know all the results of the tests yet, so he can't make a diagnosis."

"What does he suspect?" Dana was sure Mrs. Hyde was holding back some information.

"He really wouldn't say," Mr. Hyde answered, "but. . . ."

"But what, Dad? You know a lot about sickness, so you might as well tell us," Larry said.

"Larry's right, Bob. It's only fair to say what you think," Mrs. Hyde said.

Mr. Hyde took a deep breath. "There's no way to know for certain, but it could be mononucleosis. That would show up in the blood test very soon."

"That's not so bad," Shelley exclaimed. "A couple of kids had it at Canby Hall and sacked out in the infirmary for a few weeks. After that, they were good as new."

"What's the other possibility?" Dana asked.

Mr. Hyde hesitated and rubbed his forehead.

"You've got to tell us, Dad," Shelley pleaded.

"It could be meningitis." Mr. Hyde spoke in a low voice, as though he were reluctant to mention the word.

"Meningitis," Larry repeated. "That's bad news."

"That's horrible!" Shelley's voice trembled. "She could be paralyzed or blind or. . . ."

"Oh, no," Dana said softly, and the color drained from her face.

"I'm just guessing, and I probably shouldn't have said anything." Mr. Hyde shook his head, regretting that he'd upset them, perhaps unnecessarily.

"It's better to be prepared," Shelley said, seeing her father's distress. Then she added, with artificial brightness, "She's going to be all right. I just know it!"

"We've got to hope for the best. That's all we can do," Mrs. Hyde said.

At that moment, Dr. Gabriel approached and told them he'd just come from Faith's bedside.

"She's exactly the same, and I suggest you all go home and get some rest. We'll let you know if there is any change in her condition."

"She's not alone, is she?" Shelley asked.

"Not for a minute," Dr. Gabriel assured her. "We've got nurses around the clock."

"We might as well leave," Mrs. Hyde said. "There's nothing we can do now, and I'm anxious to get in touch with Faith's mother."

Everyone got up and slowly trudged toward the exit, except Dana. She hung back, waiting until the others were out of earshot, and then walked over to Dr. Gabriel.

"Faith will be okay, won't she?" Dana asked, hoping to get one shred of assurance.

"I can't promise anything," Dr. Gabriel answered. "All I can tell you is she's getting the best possible care."

"Thank you," Dana said, and turned her head so that he couldn't see her eyes misting. Then, as she hurried to catch up with the others, she thought with sudden painful awareness how much Faith and Shelley meant to her. The possibility of Faith not recovering filled her with unimaginable dread.

Shelley was waiting by the car door, and as though she had ESP, murmured with unusual seriousness, "We must never take our friendship for granted, right, Dana?"

"Right, Shel. I know now, for sure, that it's one of the most precious things in the world."

CHAPTER THIRTEEN

Shelley gave Faith's home telephone number to her mother as soon as they entered the house.

"I'll go upstairs and make the call —probably the hardest call I've ever made," she muttered as she climbed the stairs.

While she was gone, Mr. Hyde brought out a pitcher of cider from the refrigerator and poured a glass for everyone. Then he flipped on the television and said, "We need a distraction."

No one was interested in the local news that was being reported, but the noise filled the room and prevented them from expressing their worst fears. As soon as Mrs. Hyde came downstairs, which was ten minutes later, Shelley turned down the volume.

"What did she say, Mom?" Shelley asked.

"She's flying out tomorrow. She's a social worker, you know, and even though it's Sunday she can call her supervisor and make arrangements to have her cases covered. There's a direct flight from Washington to Des Moines on United Airlines that gets in about six. Of course we'll meet her."

"She can have my room," Dana volunteered. "I can easily sleep on the sofa."

"Joan — she insisted that I stop calling her Mrs. Thompson — was very definite about not wanting to inconvenience us," Mrs. Hyde said.

"But it would be easy for us to put her up," Shelley said.

"I told her that, but she's a little like Faith — stubborn." For the first time in hours Mrs. Hyde smiled.

"Where will she stay?" Jeff asked.

"She would like to stay in the hospital, in Faith's room, if possible."

"There's always the Prairie Arms," Mr. Hyde suggested. "I've met several men at the Rotary Club who have stayed there when they're passing through on business, and they all recommend it."

"I suppose that would be her second choice, but I can understand why she'd rather stay in the hospital. I would too. . . ." Mrs. Hyde's face clouded over, and she suddenly hurried into the kitchen.

"I'll help you, honey," Mr. Hyde said, and rushed after her, knowing his wife was on the verge of tears.

"Let's set the table," Dana said. "I can't stand not keeping busy."

"Know what you mean," Shelley agreed.

They both headed for the dining room, but then the phone rang. It was Paul, and Larry handed the phone to Shelley who muttered something about how she'd forgotten to let him know what had happened, but there hadn't been time. To ward off an explosion, the first words she spoke as she settled on a dining room chair and pulled the receiver to her ear was, "I'm sorry."

"Thought maybe you got kidnapped again," Paul kidded her.

"Not funny," Shelley said. She didn't like being reminded of the hair-raising experience she'd had last winter at Canby Hall. It was a case of mistaken identity, but she actually had been kidnapped. And she still had nightmares as a result.

"Then where were you? I couldn't get to the fair until after two, but there wasn't a sign of you or your family or your roommates." Paul was obviously bewildered.

"Faith's really sick," Shelley said, and then described in detail what had happened.

"I'll come over," Paul said, when she had finished, "if you want me."

"Of course I want you," Shelley answered. And as she slowly hung up the receiver, she realized how important Paul was in her life. She wondered if any boy could ever mean as much to her. She loved Paul, and needed him, and felt more confused than ever at the thought that they might break up because of Tom. But Tom was great, too. Sometimes, Shelley thought, sorting out her love life was just too much!

For the rest of the evening the phone didn't stop ringing. First it was Jed Jensen, who wanted Jeff; then the man who had been in charge of the drugstore telephoned Larry to find out why he hadn't dropped by, as promised, in the late afternoon; after that it was Cary who called to ask Shelley what she was wearing to the square dance; then a friend of Mrs. Hyde's called to congratulate her on winning a prize for her pecan pie. These calls triggered more calls, and eating dinner was a constant series of interruptions. Ordinarily the ringing phone would have been an annoyance, but even Mr. Hyde appreciated the disruption. They were on dessert — homemade brownies and ice cream — when the doorbell rang.

"Must be Paul," Shelley said, and jumped up.

She ran to the front door and was momentarily taken aback. "Cary, it's you!" she cried.

"Thought you might like some company," Cary said.

"But you were supposed to go to the square dance. I mean. . . ."

"Who cares about that?" Cary asked.

Shelley looked at her friend gratefully and choked up. She knew the square dance after the county fair was Pine Bluff's best, and Cary had looked forward to it all year.

"Thanks, Cary," she whispered, "Dana and I could use some cheering up."

They were still standing at the door when Paul arrived. "Nice to have a welcoming committee," Paul remarked, and gave each girl a kiss on the cheek. He had just the right amount of warmth and good humor for the occasion, and Shelley knew, more than ever, why she'd always love him.

Dana wasn't sure how she and Shelley got through the next hour. Even though Cary and Paul regaled her with stories about Daniel Webster Junior High and some of their exploits with Shelley, Faith was always in the back of her mind. Dana tried to appear interested, but she was relieved when they left and Shelley suggested they go back to the hospital.

"Even though we can't see Faith, I'd feel better just sitting there," Shelley said.

"I was thinking the same thing," Dana agreed.

They had purposely avoided talking about Faith all evening, but as soon as they got in the car, Shelley said in a soft, urgent voice, "She'll be all right, don't you think, Dana?"

"She just has to be," Dana replied.

They drove in silence the rest of the way, and when they arrived at the hospital, immediately asked at the information desk about Faith's condition.

After checking with the floor nurse, the

woman behind the counter told them there was no change.

"She's not any better?" Shelley asked, but she already knew the answer even before the woman shook her head.

Shelley and Dana looked at each other forlornly, and dragged themselves to the sofa and chairs at the far end of the lobby.

"I'm scared," Shelley said as she sat down. "She's getting all this care and she's not improving."

"I'm scared, too, Shel. Faith was always so strong, and Jeff said she couldn't even walk. If she doesn't get better, then. . . ."

"Is she going to die?" Shelley asked desperately.

This was the first time either of them had voiced such a terrifying thought.

"I don't know . . . I just don't know," Dana replied desolately.

"She can't," Shelley cried. "Not Faith. . . ."

"It isn't possible," Dana said.

But their firm denial of the possibility that Faith might die didn't dispel their heavy feeling of doubt. Dana could see that Shelley was on the verge of tears again, and she did her best to say something optimistic.

"Maybe tomorrow things will be better."

"Right," Shelley said. "My Dad says things always look better in the morning."

Dana was relieved that Shelley was able to contain her tears, and on the way home they both made a special effort to be cheerful. But when Dana said good-night to Shelley, all her fears returned. The sewing room was appallingly empty without Faith. Dana felt her absence more poignantly than ever, and got ready for bed like a zombie. The only bright news was that Faith's mother would be coming the next day. Joan Thompson was loving and wise, and Dana recalled how she had helped her and Shelley get over a misunderstanding that might have wrecked their friendship permanently. And she'd done it in such a gentle, unobtrusive way. Now, if she could only make things all right for Faith. . . . But Dana knew it wasn't up to Mrs. Thompson. All she could do was be there. She couldn't make Faith get well.

Dana pulled her nightshirt over her head, peeled the cover off the daybed, and collapsed. Too exhausted to wash her face and brush her teeth — a ritual she never missed — she cried herself to sleep.

The next morning when Dana went downstairs for breakfast, the entire family was in the kitchen. Mrs. Hyde was already talking to the hospital, and everyone listened intently as she spoke. She kept saying "Uh huh, Dr. Gabriel, uh huh." Then she told him that Mrs. Thompson was flying in from Washington and wanted to stay with her daughter. "She doesn't care if it's only a reclining chair, just so she can stay in the room with her," she explained. "Please see what you can do. I'll see you later."

She hung up the receiver and shook her head sadly.

"What's wrong, Mom?" Shelley tried to keep the panic out of her voice.

"There's no improvement — there's no change at all."

"At least she's not worse," Dana said, trying to bolster her own spirits.

"What's the next step?" Mr. Hyde asked.

"They're doing a spinal tap this morning, and they should get the results in a couple of hours."

"What medication is she getting?" Larry asked.

"Dr. Gabriel says until they know more, there's no specific treatment."

"What can we do?" Dana asked desperately.

"I'm afraid nothing," Mr. Hyde answered. "I think you and Shelley should try and keep busy."

"I couldn't enjoy anything as long as Faith's so sick," Shelley stated.

"Me neither." Dana was equally emphatic. "I'd like to hang out at the hospital, in case we're allowed to see her."

"I understand how you feel. I'm going over this morning, too," Mrs. Hyde said.

"Larry and I will be working on inventory today, but we can come over on a moment's notice." Mr. Hyde looked worried.

"Same with me," Jeff said. "I'm going to the farm, but Mr. Jensen said I could leave whenever I want."

"I plan to pick up Joan at the airport," Mrs. Hyde said.

"Why don't you let me do that?" Jeff asked.

"And Dana and I will go with you, Jeff," Shelley said. Then Shelley turned to her mother. "She knows us, Mom, and she doesn't need the whole family to descend on her. It might scare her."

"You're probably right, Shel. I'll wait for her at the hospital."

It wasn't until late morning that Dr. Gabriel approached Mrs. Hyde and the girls, who had been impatiently waiting for his report. They were sitting in the corner of the lobby, idly flipping through magazines, doing the crossword puzzle in the daily paper, and making a feeble attempt at small talk. The three of them tensed up visibly, and unsuccessfully tried to read his expression as he walked towards them.

"Tell us," Shelley breathed, "what's wrong with Faith?"

"The spinal tap is clear," Dr. Gabriel said, as he sat down.

"That's wonderful . . . isn't it?" Shelley exclaimed.

"It means that she doesn't have bacterial meningitis, but she does have an elevated protein level, indicating an infection."

"Does she still have such a high fever?" Mrs. Hyde asked.

"Her symptoms are the same — fever, chills, sore throat."

"What are you giving her?" Dana couldn't help asking.

"The only treatment is aspirin and fluids. Antibiotics won't help in this case. We'll just have to wait and see if further blood tests show anything new."

Dr. Gabriel stood up, indicating there was nothing further for him to report. Then he said, "Dr. Staunton will be seeing her later. And you did say her mother is coming in tonight?"

"Yes, her plane arrives at six."

"Good. We've arranged for a cot to be put in the room so that she can be close to her daughter."

"You make it sound as though she's deathly ill." Dana couldn't keep her voice from trembling.

"I don't want to alarm you, but the truth is at this point we cannot identify her disease. I can give it a fancy name — lymphocytic chorio-meningo-encephalitis — but in plain language she has an undiagnosed virus and we don't know how to treat it."

"Can't you give her something stronger than aspirin?" Mrs. Hyde inquired.

"That could be a mistake. Administering medicine that's not right can have very bad effects. Until the disease is identified, it's better to let nature take its course."

"Do you think we can look in on her?" Shelley asked.

"She might not recognize you," Dr. Gabriel answered.

"That's okay," Dana said. She was just as anxious as Shelley to see Faith.

Dr. Gabriel smiled. "I think it will make you two feel better, and it won't hurt Faith. But only for a few minutes."

"Promise," Shelley said, and waved Dana towards the elevator.

Dana and Shelley moved softly down the corridor to Room 305. They were breathing rapidly, from fear and excitement. They couldn't wait to see Faith, but they weren't sure what to expect as they tiptoed into her room. For a few seconds they stood frozen in the doorway, shocked at how ghastly Faith looked. Her usually soft cocoa skin had a mottled gray cast, and her face was gaunt. Shelley gasped and then coughed in case Faith had heard her.

"Hi," Dana said in a low voice, not sure whether Faith was sleeping or just had her eyes closed.

Faith slowly opened her eyes, and tried to smile. "This is the last place I thought I'd be spending my vacation," she muttered.

"You'll be out soon," Dana said, nervously.

"That's right." Shelley couldn't think of anything else to say.

But it didn't matter because Faith had already drifted off. Dana and Shelley looked at each other sadly, and backed out of the room.

"I'm glad her mother's coming," Shelley said as they made their way towards the elevator.

"Maybe that will help," Dana said, woefully. "Something has to. . . ."

CHAPTER FOURTEEN

It was after eight o'clock when Mrs. Thompson arrived at the hospital with Dana, Shelley, and Jeff. She was a tall, handsome woman, and even after an incredibly stressful twenty-four hours she managed to look pulled together in a navy-blue linen suit and a crisp white blouse. She was able to smile when Shelley introduced her to her parents and Larry, but she couldn't hide the terrified look in her eyes.

"I know you're anxious to see Faith, and it's all arranged so that you can stay in her room," Shelley's mother said.

"Thank you, Ann. I knew you would understand why I want to be near her. How is she?"

"The same," Mrs. Hyde answered.

"Meaning?"

"Meaning there's no change," Mr. Hyde said. "There are two doctors looking after her — Dr. Gabriel who was covering the emergency room when Jeff brought her in, and Dr. Staunton, who's the senior physician at County Hospital. Dr. Staunton told me to have him paged as soon as you arrived."

"That's so thoughtful of you. I'll feel much better when I see him . . . I hope."

"Dr. Lewis Staunton — he's famous, you know," Shelley said.

"I've never heard of him," Mrs. Thompson remarked.

"Sit down and I'll have him paged." Mr. Hyde walked over to the reception desk, while everyone tried to make small talk.

Minutes later, Dr. Staunton strode off the elevator, his spectacles balanced on his forehead. Mr. Hyde tactfully led Mrs. Thompson towards him and made the introductions. Then Faith's mother followed the doctor down the corridor into a small room, and the door was closed.

Shelley and Dana couldn't stop staring at the shut door. "The 'creeping hours of time' — Shakespeare," Shelley quoted. Dana half-smiled at Shelley's attempt to raise their flagging spirits, but neither one of them could sustain even a phony cheerfulness. And when Mrs. Thompson emerged, the frown lines on her forehead had deepened, and she seemed more worried than ever.

"I'll have a nurse show you to room 305. We've had a cot put in and I hope you'll be comfortable," the doctor said.

"Thank you, Dr. Staunton," Mrs. Thompson murmured, and stood frozen as she watched him disappear into another office.

Shelley and Dana instinctively ran up to her. "Any news?" Shelley asked.

"No. He told me everything he'd already told you."

"Then why. . . ." Shelley began, and stopped abruptly, not wanting to pry.

Mrs. Thompson smiled sadly and finished her sentence for her. "Then why do I look so troubled? Because I can't believe that her illness can't be diagnosed."

Shelley shrugged her shoulders helplessly, and Dana tried to say something comforting. "Maybe tomorrow they'll know more."

"I hope so," Mrs. Thompson said in a strained tone. "I certainly hope so."

The next forty-eight hours were a blur of nervous activity, constant anxiety, false hopes, and just plain fear. But the doctor believed that because of the enforced rest and intravenous feeding, Faith was strong enough to see her friends twice a day for ten minutes. Since their first visit, Faith had pleaded with Dr. Staunton to let her see Dana and Shelley.

"Don't wear her out," Dr. Staunton cautioned the girls the morning of the fourth day of Faith's illness, "but I think her morale will improve if she sees you two."

The girls were overjoyed that Faith had asked for them, but they took his warning to heart and went into her room cautiously. Mrs. Thompson had stayed by Faith's side ever since her arrival, but she tactfully left the room when Dana and Shelley appeared.

"You look like you shrunk," Shelley blurted out when she saw Faith lying listlessly on the pillow. Shelley had recovered from her initial shock, and was prepared to joke.

"Shelley!" Dana gasped, embarrassed by the gauche remark.

"That's okay," Faith whispered, and smiled wanly.

Then Shelley waved a pile of get-well cards at Faith. "These are mostly from the kids you met on the hayride. You read them, Dana, and I'll be in charge of decoration."

Dana read off the messages and showed the pictures to Faith before handing them to Shelley who arranged them in the mirror over the dresser. It was hard for Faith to talk, but her eyes followed her roommates in action.

Shelley and Dana laughed and kidded around, trying to keep Faith entertained. But as Dana handed the last card to Shelley, Faith said unexpectedly, "Am I going to die?"

There was a painful silence, and Dana and Shelley exchanged a desperate look. Faith was so serious, and despairing, but there was no way for her roommates to tell her the truth — that they didn't know, and it was something they didn't want to face.

"Of course not!" Shelley exclaimed. "You couldn't put us to all the trouble of finding a new roommate!"

"Shel's right," Dana said. "What a nuisance that would be!"

Faith half-smiled, and Shelley said, peering at her, "You're looking a lot better just in the few minutes we've been here, which means we are good for your morale."

"We can't stay any longer now, but we'll be back this afternoon," Dana promised.

Faith nodded her head. "Later," she breathed feebly. "I can't wait."

That afternoon Ann Hyde called Faith's mother at the hospital to inquire about Faith. She was overjoyed to hear that Shelley and Dana had been allowed to visit, and urged Mrs. Thompson to have dinner with the family.

"You need a break, Joan," she told her. "The girls will drive you here, and one of us can take you back. I promise it will be an early evening."

Mrs. Thompson hesitated. "I don't know if I. . . ."

"There's a nurse on duty to look in on Faith, and you'll only be gone a couple of hours. Please come."

"Thank you, I will," she said finally, and promptly told the girls she would be driving home with them.

When Shelley and Dana learned that Mrs.

Thompson was coming to the house, they promised each other to be cheerful. They didn't have any optimistic medical reports to go on, but at least they'd been allowed to see Faith, she was able to talk, and she'd actually smiled.

Mrs. Thompson tried to keep up a brave front, too, but she hardly touched the delicious dinner that Shelley's mother had prepared.

"You've got to keep up your strength, Joan," Ann Hyde gently admonished her, watching her pick at a chicken wing.

"I'm sorry, Ann, you've all been so nice but. . . ." Her voice faded.

"But what?" Shelley asked.

"But I want to take Faith home. I'm sure the care she is getting is fine, and. . . ."

"Do you think she should be moved?" Mr. Hyde asked.

Mrs. Thompson hesitated before she spoke.

"Have you asked Dr. Staunton?" Larry wanted to know.

Faith's mother looked uncomfortable, but it was impossible for her not to tell the truth. "I spoke to him this morning, and he doesn't advise it. And I'm not sure that the airlines will take someone who's that sick."

"Then why in the world . . ." Shelley began, but Mrs. Hyde gave her one of her "Be quiet" looks.

Shelley couldn't totally shut up, but she did change her tack. "Personally, I think she should stay here. I mean we can see her every day and. . . .'"

"And maybe we're being selfish," Dana interjected.

"She is getting excellent care," Mr. Hyde pointed out.

"I'm sure that's true," Mrs. Thompson said, "and I've never seen a friendlier staff or a cleaner hospital but. . . ." She was floundering, searching for the right words, not wanting to hurt anyone's feelings.

"But you want her to be in her hometown," Jeff said.

"That's exactly right, I want her to be in her hometown," Mrs. Thompson echoed, and smiled at Jeff appreciatively. Dana, too, smiled at Jeff and again was ashamed of herself for underestimating him. He had stood up for Faith's mother against the wishes of his family. She wondered if anyone she knew, including Bret, was so gutsy.

Mrs. Hyde, not wanting to keep her guest on the firing line, deftly shifted the conversation by asking about the Brown's new roof. It was a silly question, but everyone sensed why she was doing it, and soon there was the usual banter at the table: Jeff half-kidded about finding a proper mate for Gertrude; Larry described one of his customer's latest imaginary ailments — tingling earlobes; Mrs. Hyde revealed her secret of a perfect piecrust — generous pricking of the dough. Joan Thompson tried to follow the

lively conversation, but she was too pre-
occupied thinking about Faith. As soon as
she finished her coffee, she pushed back her
chair, indicating she wanted to leave.

"I'll take you back to the hospital," Jeff
volunteered promptly.

"Thanks, Jeff. I'm sorry to eat and run, but
I am worried about Faith."

"Do you mind if Dana and I go with you?
For some reason, we feel a lot better being
close to her, even if we can't see her."

Mrs. Thompson smiled at Shelley and
Dana fondly. "Of course you can come back
to the hospital." She added, "I can see why
Faith considers you her best friends."

Then she thanked the Hydes and rushed
out. Once they were in the car, she immediately confided her plans.

"I've spoken to my supervisor whose husband is on the staff of George Washington
University Hospital. That's one of the best
hospitals in D.C., and he's promised to get
Faith a bed there. Your folks just don't
understand."

"We all want to do what's best for Faith,"
Jeff said.

"I know that, so you've got to help me.
I'd like to check her out of the hospital
tomorrow and get her to Washington — by
train, if necessary."

"But that's such a long trip!" Shelley said.

"I know that, but if the airlines won't take
her. . . ." Her voice broke.

Jeff realized that Mrs. Thompson was distraught — and determined. No amount of reasoning would help. If the doctor couldn't persuade her to keep Faith in County Hospital until she was well, then no one could.

When they arrived at the hospital, Jeff, Dana, and Shelley waited in the lobby while Mrs. Thompson went to check on Faith.

"I'll be right back and tell you how she is," she told them as she headed for the elevator.

Minutes later she returned, looking more upset than ever. "She's worse," she mumbled. "Hasn't opened her eyes since I left, and her temperature has shot up. And I was only gone a short time." She began to weep openly.

"Is the doctor coming?" Shelley asked.

"He's already looked at her, and the nurse is with her now. But she's worse," Mrs. Thompson repeated, her face flooded with tears. "I've got to get her home."

Dana put her arms around her, and tried to comfort her, while Shelley handed her a fistful of tissues.

"I'll do what I can to help you," Jeff said. "And I'm sure my folks will, too."

"Thank you," Mrs. Thompson said, gaining control of her emotions. "Even if they disapprove, I have to do what I think is right. Imagine if you hadn't followed your instincts when you found Faith, almost unconscious. . . ."

❋   ❋   ❋

Back at the house, since it was no longer necessary to keep up Mrs. Thompson's spirits, a cloud of depression settled over everyone. Jeff knew his announcement wouldn't do anything to alleviate the gloom that pervaded the room, but he wanted to get it over with.

"I promised Faith's mother I'd help get her and Faith home as soon as possible." Jeff sat down on the sofa next to Dana.

"But don't you think . . . ?" Shelley began.

"It's not our decision," Mrs. Hyde said.

"She has to do what she thinks best," Mr. Hyde stated. "And while you were at the hospital, I checked with the airlines. There's no way they'll take a stretcher case with an unidentified illness."

"And she's acting against the advice of the doctor so she won't get an official release," Larry said.

"A bus trip is out of the question, and I think the train ride would be a nightmare. This is awful," Jeff groaned.

"There must be some way, Bob." Mrs. Hyde looked beseechingly at her husband. "Isn't there somebody you know who could help her?"

"Wait a minute," Mr. Hyde said, "wait a minute. There is somebody who just might. Gerald Simpson could be the answer."

"You mean the rancher with a thousand acres of land south of the valley?" Jeff asked, his face brightening.

"That's exactly who I mean," Mr. Hyde said. "He's got a private plane, a company plane that he uses to fly himself and his associates around the country."

"Do you think he might offer it and his pilot?" Shelley's eyes gleamed.

"Gerry's an old friend, and a very nice guy. I'm going to tell him the situation, and see what he says. The plane and the pilot may not be available now, but there's no harm in trying."

"It's a long shot, Dad, but if it works. . . ." Jeff sighed hopefully.

Mr. Hyde went upstairs to make the call, and the others waited nervously.

"If there's room — and he'll offer the plane — I'd like to fly back with them," Dana said.

"You're leaving me, Dana?" Shelley cried.

"I think it'll be easier on Faith if I leave now, and maybe I can help Mrs. Thompson somehow, if she wants me."

"You're probably right," Shelley sighed, "but I'll sure miss you."

"Me too," Jeff murmured, so that only Dana could hear.

"What a bummer this vacation turned into," Shelley groaned. "It started out so great, and now. . . ." Her face contorted, and she burst into tears.

"Why don't you come back with us?" Dana said. "It'll be a free ride, and Faith would feel better knowing we're all together."

"Could I go, Mom?" Shelley asked, brushing her tears away.

"I don't see why not," her mother answered thoughtfully. And then she added, "Providing we get the plane, and if Faith's mother would like you to go."

Just then, Mr. Hyde appeared, a wide smile spreading across his face.

"Success!" he shouted. "Gerry says we can have the plane. In fact, he says he's thrilled to put it to such good use."

"Is there room for me and Dana, too?" Shelley held her breath. "We want to go back with Faith."

"I figured that," Mr. Hyde said. "There's enough room for all of you."

"How big is it?" Jeff asked.

"It's a corporate jet — seats six, including the pilot. The backseats are removable, so there'll be room for a stretcher."

"What time does it leave, and from where?" Mrs. Hyde wanted to know.

"We should be at the Globe Building at Des Moines Airport at ten o'clock tomorrow morning."

"I'll call Mrs. Thompson right now." Jeff was elated. "She'll never believe it!"

CHAPTER FIFTEEN

W e'll be ready and waiting," Mrs. Thompson said excitedly when Jeff told her about the flight plans. "I have a million things to do — check us out, make arrangements for Faith's sister to meet us at the airport, call my supervisor about reserving a bed in George Washington University Hospital. . . ."

"Dana and Shelley want to go with you. Is that okay?" Jeff asked.

"I'd love them to," Mrs. Thompson replied. "Now I better get started." She hung up without saying good-bye.

Jeff returned the receiver to the hook and slowly made his way upstairs. Dana's door was open, and she had begun to pack her suitcase which was on the bed.

"Can't believe you're actually leaving," Jeff said, leaning against the doorframe. "And I'm responsible for getting you out of here so fast." He no longer felt exuberant about his accomplishment, and wondered if he had done the right thing.

"You did what you had to do," Dana said, sensing his turmoil. "I think you were wonderful."

"Do you think I'll ever see you again?"

"Who knows?" Dana believed in her heart of hearts that although he meant a lot to her, Jeff was a summer romance and it wouldn't be fair to encourage him.

"I have something I want you to have — so you don't forget me," he said. "Don't go away."

He hurried down the hall and returned in a flash, holding a small package elaborately wrapped in the memorable general store paper.

"For me?" she asked. Her thoughts had been far away, concerned with Faith and the unknown future.

"Open it," Jeff said.

Dana frowned curiously at the box — too big for jewelry, too small for clothing — and slowly unwrapped it. She opened the box and gasped when she saw a small stuffed cow that bore an amazing resemblance to Gertrude.

"It's adorable!" she exclaimed. "No one has ever given me a cow before."

"You're the only girl I would have given one to. Promise me whenever you look at her, you'll think of me, will you?"

"I'll never forget you, Jeff, never." Then

she threw her arms around him and hugged him with a kind of affection that she'd never felt for any boy.

The logistics of getting everyone to the airport worked out without a flaw. Faith, accompanied by her mother, was transported on a stretcher by ambulance, and Mr. Hyde drove the others in the station wagon. But no one could ease the pain of saying good-bye.

Kevin, the pilot of the private plane, was a sandy-haired Irishman who inspired confidence. He had already fueled up the gas tank, and arranged for the backseats to be removed. Everyone was hovering around Faith, who was totally out of it, and it was a blessing that Kevin cut short what would have been a prolonged farewell.

"We have to board right away," he said, "since we have a limited amount of time in which to take off. If we miss our departure time we may be delayed for hours."

That galvanized everyone into action. First Larry and Jeff helped load the stretcher on the plane. Mr. and Mrs. Hyde blew a kiss to Faith, even though they knew she was completely unaware of their gesture. Then there was a rapid exchange of embraces, words of encouragement, and expressions of gratitude. Jeff, knowing this might be his last chance to ever see Dana, ignored the fact that he had an audience, put his arms around her, and kissed her good-bye. He couldn't bring himself to say anything, but before he let her go he gently squeezed her shoulders.

"We really have to leave," Kevin said, and held the door for Dana. The others had already boarded.

Dana moved towards the plane and turned around. She had shown remarkable restraint up to that point, but as she looked at the Hydes, she was overwhelmed with feelings of affection and an unexpected sense of loss at leaving them, and she couldn't help the two tears that spilled down her cheeks. She waved good-bye and tried to smile, and then ducked rapidly into the plane.

"What's the matter?" Shelley asked, as Dana sat down in the seat next to her. She could see that Dana was crying for real now.

"You'll never believe this," she answered, only half-kidding, "but I think I'm already homesick for Pine Bluff."

Mrs. Thompson had arranged for an ambulance to meet them when they landed, and Sarah was also at the airport. Sarah kissed her mother, and enthusiastically hugged Shelley and Dana, whom she'd gotten to know when the girls had visited the Thompsons one weekend during the school year. She started to ask them about their flight, but then she saw Faith, skeletonlike, being carried off the plane on the stretcher by Kevin and the ambulance attendant. Her blood froze.

"Mother," Sarah cried, "she looks . . . she looks awful!"

"I should have warned you," Mrs. Thompson said somberly.

"But she doesn't look like Faith . . . she's barely recognizable."

"I know, dear. That's why we're here — that's why we flew back. . . ."

Sarah ran up to the stretcher, spoke softly to Faith, and grasped her hand. There was no response — Faith's eyes remained closed and her hand was limp.

"Mother . . ." Sarah said, "she's so sick." Sarah's eyes began to tear, but she knew her mother needed her to be strong. She couldn't allow herself to fall apart. "Mother, what do you want me to do?"

"The best thing would be to take the girls back to the house, while I get Faith settled in the hospital. My supervisor's brother has arranged for Dr. Green, a diagnostic specialist, to be in charge of the case. That's such a relief. . . ." Mrs. Thompson couldn't help believing that now Faith would get the kind of treatment that only a hospital in the East could provide. "I'll call you later," she said, as she followed the stretcher into the ambulance.

* * *

The Thompsons lived on the second floor of a four-story house with a wide front stoop. Sarah showed Dana and Shelley to Richie's room where they had stayed before, and they felt right at home with the pennants, posters of football stars, and tanks of fish.

Sarah sat on one of the twin beds while Dana and Shelley unpacked and answered all her questions. Sarah, whom Faith had always described as the cool member of the family, understandably broke down when she learned the details of Faith's illness.

"And my mother thinks that here they might find the answers?"

"That's what she's hoping," Shelley said.

"I hope she's right," Sarah sighed, and stood up. "Now I better go wash my face. The last thing I want is for her to see me unhinged."

She was halfway out the door when she turned around and asked, "Does Johnny Bates know about this?"

"Not yet," Shelley said, "but I think he should."

"I think we should call him," Dana agreed, "if it's okay with you, Sarah."

"I think Faith would want him to know. If anything happens. . . ." She turned quickly then, not wanting anyone to see her cry again.

As soon as Sarah had left, Shelley said, "You call him, Dana. I'll fall apart."

"Might as well get it over with," Dana said.

"But you come give me moral support. There's a phone in the kitchen."

Shelley followed Dana, and slumped down in a chair at the kitchen table while Dana called the information operator for Johnny's number and then dialed.

"What's wrong?" Johnny asked, as soon as he heard Dana's voice.

As gently as possible, Dana told him the reason for her call.

"I'll come to Washington," Johnny said when she was finished.

Dana could hear the anguish in his voice, and knew how helpless he felt. But traveling to Washington wouldn't help Faith. "No, Johnny. I don't think you should . . . not yet."

"But why?"

"Because she's unconscious, and she won't even know you're here."

"I can't do anything to help?"

"When she's feeling better, but right now Shelley and I are here. And we're trying to look after Mrs. Thompson. I promise you we'll let you know if anything changes."

"I suppose you're right," Johnny said reluctantly. "But promise you'll tell me everything. I'll call you tomorrow."

When Dana hung up, Shelley said, "You were right to talk him out of coming until later, when she gets better." She hesitated. "If she does get better."

"We have to think positive," Dana said.

"We'll all be back at Canby Hall in a few weeks."

"You and I will, but what about Faith?"

"Look, Shel, she's in a different hospital, that has all the best equipment, and Mrs. Thompson has the finest doctor taking care of her. I'm sure they'll find a way to cure her."

"And what if they don't, Dana? What then?"

"I don't want to think about it." Dana and Shelley looked at each other despondently. There was nothing else to say and Dana was afraid they'd both start to cry when they heard the front door open.

"Hello, anybody home?" Mrs. Thompson asked in a strained voice.

Shelley and Dana ran into the living room to greet her. "How is she?" they asked in unison.

"No change. Dr. Green has seen her, and they're making more tests. We have to wait until tomorrow for the results."

"Let me fix you some tea," Shelley said. "You look exhausted."

"I am," Mrs. Thompson admitted, as she sank down on the sofa. Then she managed to smile. "The only good part about today is that you two girls and Sarah are here."

The next couple of days were an ongoing nightmare. Faith was still unconscious and her fever raged. There were frantic phone calls from Johnny in Greenleaf, and the

Hydes in Pine Bluff. Everyone was hoping desperately for reassurance, but the tests confirmed the diagnosis that had been made in the hospital in Iowa — a virus.

The hospital in Washington was run with impersonal efficiency. Shelley and Dana weren't allowed to look in on Faith, but they went to the hospital every day and sat with Mrs. Thompson and Sarah in the waiting room. Every morning Dr. Green, after making his rounds, would consult with Mrs. Thompson. He was a distinguished, gray-haired man, who abruptly told her the progress — or lack of progress — Faith was making.

"But there's nothing else you can do?" Mrs. Thompson pleaded, after hearing the same report three days in a row.

"Absolutely nothing. The results of our tests corroborate those we received from County Hospital in Iowa. Faith was given the proper treatment there, and we are continuing it."

Then he rushed off, and there was nothing for Mrs. Thompson and the girls to do but wait. That night, after visiting hours, they went home as usual. Usually they grabbed a bite in a nearby coffee shop, but Shelley and Dana insisted on making dinner. Shelley had prepared lasagna, and Dana was going to try Mrs. Hyde's apple pie recipe. Sarah was setting the table while Mrs. Thompson tried to watch the news on TV, when the phone rang.

Shelley impulsively picked up the receiver, and trying to keep her voice calm, told Mrs. Thompson that Dr. Green was calling her. Everyone stopped what they were doing and the quiet was excruciating as Faith's mother ran to the phone. They all knew this was a life-or-death report.

"Yes," Mrs. Thompson breathed, almost inaudibly. "Yes," she repeated, and her eyes began tearing, but she was smiling at the same time. Then she listened some more, nodding her head all the while, and finally said, "Thank you, Dr. Green, thank you."

"Tell us!" Shelley shouted, even before Mrs. Thompson had hung up the receiver. "Tell us!"

"The crisis has passed," Mrs. Thompson said in a trembling voice. "Faith opened her eyes tonight, her fever is almost normal, and the first thing she asked for was pretzels and mustard."

They all began laughing and crying at the same time, grabbed each other, shouted with joy, and made Mrs. Thompson repeat over and over exactly what Dr. Green had said.

"She must feel okay if she feels like pretzels and mustard," Shelley said.

"We'll see for ourselves tomorrow. Dr. Green says she'll be ready for visitors — one at a time."

"I've got to let my family know," Shelley said. "And we should call Johnny."

"I'd like to call your folks, Shelley," Mrs.

Thompson said. "I've had plenty of time to think lately, and I realize how wonderful they were to me and Faith. I was so worried about her that I couldn't think straight, but I realize what Jeff sacrificed for her; how good the doctors and the hospital were in Iowa; how incredibly kind it was of Mr. Simpson to let us have his plane."

"That's the way we are in Pine Bluff," Shelley remarked, trying to sound casual. But her eyes twinkled, and there was no way she could hide her feeling of pride.

The next morning the girls took turns paying a visit to Faith. They were only allowed to spend ten minutes with her, and Dana was the last one to drop in. Her heart was racing as she walked softly into the room, afraid of how Faith would look. But Faith was sitting up in bed; her eyes were bright; and she motioned Dana closer so that she could hold her hand.

"How are you?" Dana asked, knowing it was an idiotic question.

"I'm fine — I mean I'm almost fine. I feel like a worn-out laundry sack, but the doctor and Mom tell me I'll be perfect very soon."

"Do you remember what happened to you in Pine Bluff?"

"Everything — Jeff practically carrying me to the hospital, the doctors and nurses — everything. And Mom tells me they made the right diagnosis. They repeated all those dumb

tests here and came up with the same answers. Can you believe that?"

"They were super there."

"I guess we learned a lot about small town
life in a very short time. People there were
so great."

"And we were such snobs! I'm ashamed of
myself."

"Me, too. They took such good care of
me. . . ."

"You'll be back at school on time, won't
you?"

"Of course I will! You already told me how
inconsiderate I'd be to make my best friends
find a new roommate. Besides, I'm irre-
placeable!"

"That sounds like the old Faith," Dana
said, laughing.

"No," Faith said thoughtfully. "A small
town has made a new Faith out of me. We
really were so rotten, Dana. So superior, just
because we came from Eastern cities."

Dana nodded in agreement. "I know. Pine
Bluff has a lot New York doesn't have.
Mostly, a lot of people who care about each
other, and even care about strangers."

"Well, maybe we can go back next summer and get to the county fair," Faith said
laughing. "I know one boy who would like
that."

Dana smiled, somewhat shyly for Dana.
"Jeff?"

Faith said, "Why not?"

"I think I'm off boys for good. Even great guys like Jeff. I don't seem to handle relationships very well."

Then Dana looked at the door to the hospital room carefully and dug into her tote. "I brought you something." She handed Faith a wrapped package.

Faith opened it and took out a huge, soft pretzel covered with mustard. "Now I know who the perfect roommate is."

"I could have told you that before," Dana said and she reached over and covered one of Faith's hands with her own. "I've missed you, Faithie. I'm glad you're okay."

Faith's eyes filled for a moment. "I told you I'd never leave you and Shel to some strange, creepy roommate."

Shelley stuck her head in the door. "You have to go, Dana. They'll come after you in a second." But she came into the room and the three girls held hands and looked at each other. "We're the best," Shelley said.

"But of course," Faith answered in a bright, strong voice.